RUNAWAY FAE

A VAMPIRE HUNTRESS CHRONICLES NOVELLA

JESSICA WAYNE

B.A.D.
PUBLISHING

PRAISE FOR JESSICA WAYNE'S FANTASY NOVELS

A TETHERED DUET

"Gets you all in your feel goods."
-BlueEyedCtryGirl (Amazon Reviewer)

"To me, "home" is a sense of belonging and being in your place in the world. It isn't just the house and neighborhood you live in -- it is also the people in your life. Throughout the story, these characters found their home, took care of it, returned home, and fought for home"
-Deb's hooked on books (Amazon Reviewer)

COLLATERAL DAMAGE

"Oh, what a ride! The author did a brilliant job with a first scene, getting us emotionally involved in Timothy's backstory."
-Jamie (Amazon Reviewer)

"A hard to put down story of magic, revenge and love."
-NanaPat (Amazon Reviewer)

WARRIOR OF MAGICK

"High fantasy at its best, Jessica Wayne effortlessly

paints an epic picture filled with tense romance, rich friendships, and an explosive plot. Read now or regret it!"
-*Kelly St. Clare, USA Today Bestselling Author*

"This book starts off with a bang and just keeps on rolling--right to an awesome end that leaves you hanging by your fingertips!"
-*Deb B (Amazon Reviewer)*

RISE OF THE PHOENIX

"Anastasia and Dakota take you on emotional read of love, loss, action, adventure and sometimes heartbreak."
-*Cynthia (Amazon Reviewer)*

"It will hit you in all the feels!"
-*Rose (Amazon Reviewer)*

"This book is filled with action, fight for power, and a love that can beat all odds."
-*Bri-Anna J. (Amazon Reviewer)*

"A fantastic next-in-series…"
-*Bella (Amazon Reviewer)*

"This story is full of action, magic, suspense and so

many emotions to have your heart beating a mile a minute."
-Bibliophile Babes Book Blog

"Want to see a heroine kick some booty? Read the Phoenix series in full, and MAKE SURE you finish with the Sorceress."
-Amazon Reviewer

"...action packed from beginning to end."
-Amanda (Amazon Reviewer)

"Jessica has such a creative mind and she always does an amazing job putting that creativity into her writing."
-Heather (Amazon Reviewer)

"This book was jam-packed with action and suspense! It was such a terrific ending to an amazing series! I highly recommend reading this entire series! If I could give this book more than 5 stars I would!"
-Heather (Amazon Reviewer)

"Amazing read with lots of twist and turns and everything will be revealed for an awesome ending that you won't want to miss!"
-Cynthia (Amazon Reviewer)

To the original Rachel.
Thank you for being such a badass friend. Here's that fae I
promised you.

RUNAWAY FAE

B.A.D.
PUBLISHING

Runaway Fae
A Vampire Huntress Chronicles Novella
By Jessica Wayne
Copyright © 2021. All rights reserved.

Edited by Dawn
Proofread by Rachel Cass
Cover Design by Carol Marques

❧ Created with Vellum

CONTENTS

PROLOGUE
RACHEL

I run, a full sprint between the buildings. My lungs burn while my muscles scream in pain. I have literally no idea where I'm going or if I'm even anywhere near an exit, but I can't give up. If I have to run until my feet fall off, I'll do it.

My foot catches on uneven asphalt, and I stumble forward. The side of my face slams into the concrete, and pain explodes at the points of contact. Warm blood trickles from the wounds as I scramble to my feet, trying like hell to keep moving.

"I can smell your blood," he calls out. "Delicious."

He's too close. I choke on a sob and duck back into the shadows.

I'm surrounded.

There's nowhere to go.

Nowhere to run.

The alley around me begins to spin, and I close my eyes to shove the panic-induced vertigo at bay. My body heats, and sweat beads at my temples as I repeat over and over again, *please don't see me.*

If they find me, I'm dead. But what's worse is that Ridley will suffer. After everything he's done for me, he will ultimately be the one to pay the price for my stupidity.

Pain, torture, mental torment, I'll take all of it if it means saving him from what I know is coming. Except, I also know my death will lead to his own.

I try again to free my wrists from the iron shackles binding them together. Every movement sends fresh pain up through my forearm, and struggling proves to be useless. The shackles are tight, further cementing what I fear will soon happen.

All because I was desperate for my freedom. Freedom that I always had—until now.

"Little fae, come out, come out wherever you are!" the woman calls out, her throaty voice amused. "We have so much to discuss!"

"Our time together is nowhere near done!" the man calls out.

I know he's right. Defeated, I tuck my knees up and

remain silent, knowing the one good thing is that if they're here, Max is safe.

For now.

So here I sit, hoping, praying, my silent pleas the only company I have as I remain hidden from view.

But for how long? How long can I keep playing this sadistic game of cat and mouse? I shut my eyes tightly, and tears burn in the corners as I recall every choice, every moment that led me here. The domino effect that was initiated with a single gunshot wound to the chest.

Then my life was simple, ordinary, leading me to ask the one burning question I feel horrible for even considering—why the hell couldn't he just let me stay dead?

CHAPTER ONE

RACHEL

TWO WEEKS EARLIER

The coffee cup warming my hand is barely noted as I stare blankly ahead. One night. One freaking night and my entire world was flipped upside down. No, not just upside down. It was turned inside out, flipped onto its head, and spun around in multiple circles until it was so disoriented that there was no telling which way was left and which was right.

"Can I get you anything else, hun?"

I glance up at the barista who'd introduced herself as Shanice. Her kind, dark eyes narrow on my face when I don't instantly answer, and her brow furrows in concern.

She leans down, eyes darting side to side as if she's looking for the source of my anxiety. "You okay?"

I swallow hard. *No, I lost my job, my life, and my entire damned existence in one afternoon.* "Just tired, thanks." Forcing a smile, I hold up my coffee mug. "I'll take another one of these, though."

She returns the gesture, though just like mine, hers is forced. I know she doesn't believe me, but thankfully, she doesn't press before taking my mug and turning away.

This city is the only place I've been able to hide from *him*. At least, for the last forty-eight hours. I've been to dozens of other states, my hometown, the city I went to medical school—and he's tracked me down every time.

Honestly, there's no telling how much longer I have before he manages to track me here, too.

I shut my eyes as the image of the dark-haired fae pops into my mind. His handsome smile, near-golden eyes… they haunt my every waking moment. Hell, they haunt my dreams. Not a restful minute anywhere to be seen for me.

Somehow, we're connected. Tied together in some screwed-up way I don't even want to bother looking into. Even now I can feel his panic, his anger, as he searches for me. Compliments of the bond forced upon us by some unseen entity in the Veil—the place I went after my human self was shot and killed, collateral damage in a supernatural war I'd jumped headfirst into.

Most of the time, I carefully plan everything. Consequences, worst-case scenarios—all that noise. But no, the one time I likely should have weighed the risk, I jumped head-first in—and it killed me.

Why Ridley came in after me I do not understand, though he told me, when he'd found me hiding out in California, that he'd come for me because the thought of my life being snuffed out was too horrific to bear.

Too horrific. I snort into my mug. I'd pay good money to bet it was actually because his magical boner for my human self had been what was too much to bear.

My throat tightens. I wanted a normal life. A husband, kids, white-picket-fence, and what did I get? Death, rebirth, and a fae stalker. Super fun combination if you ask me.

"Here you go, hun." Shanice returns and places the steaming mug in front of me again.

"Thanks."

"You know, I have a friend who has a brother on the police force. If you are in trouble—"

I wish you could help me. "No trouble, just tired."

"You sure?"

7

No. "Yes." I force a smile. "How long have you had this place?"

She straightens. "I opened it a few years back, wanted to work for myself."

"That's so great. And in such a big city, too."

She glances out the front windows, a wistful look on her face. "I love this crazy place. Lived near here my entire life. Where are you from?"

"Montana."

Her eyes widen, and I can all but see her excitement radiating around her. She bends over at the waist and rests her elbows on the countertop. "Did you hear what happened in Billings two months ago?"

I snort. Hear about it? I was right smack-dab in the center of it. "Why do you think I left?"

She leans in closer before glancing quickly at the patron working quietly on his computer a few seats to my left. "Do you believe they're real?"

Not seeing what harm a half-truth could do at this point, I nod. "I absolutely do."

Shanice grins widely in victory. I'd be willing to bet more than one person has told her she's crazy even though supernaturals have been all over the damned news lately. "Have you ever seen one?"

Enough for a lifetime. My thoughts drift back to the hunters, witches, shifters, and fae I spent days and nights with while we fought back against a council bent on destroying them. "I wouldn't know for sure," I lie smoothly and get to my feet. Reaching into the back pocket of my jeans, I withdraw a twenty and slide it across the counter. "Thanks for the coffee."

"You're welcome. Come back anytime!" she calls out as I step onto the busy street, trading the delicate aroma of freshly baked goods for that of car exhaust and wet concrete after last night's storm.

I've got no cell phone, no way to call and check in with the hospital to attempt and extend the leave of absence I took after vampires attacked and killed nearly half a dozen humans, and returning home right now is just not an option.

I need time. Space. And there's no damned way Ridley will give me either if I go back to Billings.

My throat tightens as tears burn the corners of my eyes. I'm alive, and even if I don't understand what I am now or this unwanted connection I have with Ridley, simply drawing breath is something—right?

Though, to be entirely honest, I would have rather just stayed dead.

A car honks, and someone sticks their middle finger out the window as a yellow cab pulls onto the busy street. Around me, humans walk, some headed home after a long night of partying, others on their way to work, all of them what I used to be—*normal.*

Damn, what I'd give for that simplicity again.

The air around me shifts, and the hairs on the back of my neck stand on end. I stiffen, already knowing what's about to happen.

"Where the bloody hell have you been?" His deep

voice washes over me, sending my heart racing. The magic in my blood—so alien to me—rushes forward, warming me like a temperate bath as it responds to him.

Turning, I face the man I've been running from for the last two months. We've crossed paths more than once. Hell, he managed to track me down daily until I came here. Ridley's eyes narrow on my face, and for the first time since I met the fae, he actually looks as exhausted as I feel.

Guilt washes over me, a solid punch to the gut because I know it's my fault. He brought me back to life, and I've repaid him by running from it.

"Here." I turn and begin to walk down the street, knowing he will follow me. The new tattoos on my arms—yet another change courtesy of dying and being brought back—tingle, and I wonder if he feels it, too. After all, he's sporting a matching set.

"Are you okay?" he asks as soon as we're alone.

I whirl on him. "Do you care?" My demand is empty, though, because I know he thinks he does. Even as he was pissed when his magic bonded to me in my human form, he was determined to care, to keep me safe.

What's really fucked up about this whole situation, though, is that he can love no other, and I don't want him.

What a pair we are.

"Are you serious? What the bloody hell do you

think I've been doing for the last two months?"

"Stalking me, obviously." I turn.

"Everyone is worried about you. Bronywyn—"

My friend's name weighs heavily on my shoulders. I know she must be worried, but honestly, her hands are full enough with the supernatural outing and new council formation to deal with. "Bronywyn is busy enough. I doubt she needs me."

His hand wraps around my arm, and I try to ignore the rush I feel at the contact. The warmth that spreads from his touch and through the rest of my body.

Damn this magical bond. I turn toward him. "Let. Me. Go."

"No. Not until you promise to stop running long enough so we can talk."

"What is there to talk about?" I shoot back. "I didn't ask for this bond, and frankly, you're an arrogant ass I want nothing to do with."

He moves in closer, his hand tightening until it's near painful. "No? Then why is your heart hammering in your chest?" He steps in even closer, standing only a handful of inches from me now. "And if you want nothing to do with me, why is it you came running to me in the Veil? Your arms wrapped around me was a really funny way of avoiding me."

I swallow hard. "I had just died. People do crazy shit when they die."

His expression darkens. "You have to stop running."

"No, I don't." I rip my arm from his grasp and

picture my apartment. As soon as I do, magic rushes through me, and I dematerialize. The world falls away briefly until, less than a second later, I'm standing in my apartment.

The moment my feet are back on the ground, I take a deep, steadying breath, my futile attempt at calming my heart. I have maybe seconds before he shows back up, but as I wait, I study the apartment that I've spent the last seven years of my life in.

Throw pillows boasting quotes about happiness and sunshine line my white couch while pictures from my otherwise happy life cover the walls. How many years did I spend overseas in dangerous areas, treating patients with Doctors Without Borders?

And yet it was a supernatural gunning me down inside a warehouse that took me out.

The air shifts around me, and I shudder, the precursor for Ridley's sudden appearance behind me.

"Rachel," he whispers my name, the pain in his tone more than apparent. I hate that it guts me. That I feel a sense of guilt when it comes to him.

I never wanted any of this.

"Please look at me."

I shake my head as tears slip down my cheeks, escapees I wish would have stayed the hell put. I've spent months crying, and I don't want to do it anymore.

Ridley appears in front of me. "Please just talk to me."

This time, I do look up at him. "About what, Ridley? I feel like we've pretty well covered how I feel."

"We aren't done yet. We can't be done talking yet."

"Why the hell not?" Angrily, I wipe the tears away. "You made this choice for me."

His cheeks flush with color, and his eyes glow brightly with power. "Would you rather I leave you dead?"

My answer is an easy one. "Yes."

He turns away from me, jaw tight, then spins back around. "You know, I never pegged you for a coward."

"A coward?" I take an angry step forward. "Are you serious?"

"Being dead would have been easy, right? Because coming back as something more powerful than you were before takes some getting used to."

"I am not a coward," I growl back even as I know he's right. Death would be easier because there would be no caring about any of this, no feelings for the fae before me, and no anger at the lack of control I now have over my own future.

"Sure as fuck could have fooled me."

We stand there within the air snapping around us with the force of our anger. "You stole my choice."

"Did you choose to get shot? Did you choose to die? Because in case you forgot, it wasn't me who stole that fucking choice from you. It was the bastard who pulled the mother fucking trigger."

Logically, I know he's right. I know it wasn't his

13

fault, but this? This is too much. It's all too much. My entire body feels one sneeze away from being a nuclear bomb. The power in my veins, I don't understand it.

And dematerializing? While I may seem to have that under control, it's terrifying. The first time I tried to get to New York, I ended up appearing underwater, so far down I thought I was going to drown.

"Don't pretend for a second that you brought me back for me. You brought me back because of *you*. Because it was the easiest decision for *you*."

He jumps back as if I struck him. Shit, maybe I should.

"Are you fucking kidding me, woman? Easy? You think chasing you all over the fucking world is *easy?* I'm just glad you haven't figured out how to get to Faerie yet, or I'd likely never have found you."

"Now there's an idea!" I scream back.

He narrows his eyes at me. "You may want to keep fooling yourself that I only brought you back because it was easy, but you couldn't be more wrong." His tone has shifted, dropped to little more than a growl. "Being tethered to you? It's not what I wanted in any damned scenario. I brought you back, not just because my magic claimed you as its other half but because the idea of your body rotting in some wooden box killed me. The very thought of your fiery soul being snuffed out was far too horrific an idea to bear. If you want nothing to do with me, fine; I'll leave you the fuck alone, but don't cheapen what I did because you're too much of a coward to face it yourself." He reaches into his pocket and withdraws my cell, tosses it onto the couch, and disappears.

I swallow hard and stare at the photo he'd been standing in front of. Me surrounded by a tribe in South Africa, all of us smiling. For some reason, that memory comes rushing back to me. We'd been held at gunpoint an hour before that photo was taken, and while I'd been terrified, that terror was nothing compared to what I feel now.

Not because it was any less of a life-or-death situation but because, in that moment, I knew what I was: human. A woman willing to die for what she believed in. For her calling.

Now I have no damned clue what I am. Fae? Human? A mixture of both?

What's worse than that, though, is the feeling that I have no choice in where I'm supposed to go from here.

Be with the arrogant fae? Or remain alone for what will likely be all of eternity?

And if I choose the latter, can I condemn us both?

CHAPTER TWO

RIDLEY

"**B**loody fucking women."

"Rachel troubles?" Fearghas questions from his couch as I plop down beside him.

"You know, you'd fucking think she'd be grateful I didn't let her stay dead. But, no, she's bloody pissed and claims I brought her back for my own fucking joy."

The other fae chuckles and shakes his head. "You did bring her back for you, though, didn't you?"

I glare at him. "Why does everyone think I'm so fucking selfish?"

"It's in our nature," he replies easily. "Your magic claimed her, did it not?" He stands and moves across his apartment to the kitchen, so I follow, ignoring the ache in my chest that appears whenever I'm too far from Rachel. *Bloody frustrating woman.*

"Doesn't mean that's the only reason I brought her back. Hell, letting her die would have been easier."

"Did you tell her that?"

"Fuck no."

"Why?" his simple question makes me want to ram my fist into his jaw.

"Could you let Eira die?" Referencing the siren my fae companion is in love with is a low blow, yes, but that's all I have these days. And the fact that he's also in love with a woman who wants nothing to do with him means we're on the same fucking page.

Same damned paragraph.

His eyes flash with power moments before he shakes his head and leans back against the counter. "No. No, I couldn't."

"Even if it was what she wanted?"

He shakes his head. "Not even then." He sighs, shoulders slumping. "I'm not saying I don't understand why you brought her back, but you should probably be honest with her about the reason."

"I was."

"Then tell her the truth. That her death as a human would have freed you from the link your magic made with her."

"I can't do that." After running both hands over my face, I lean back against the island opposite to where he's standing.

"Why not?"

"You didn't see her, the way she looked at me, such hatred. If I tell her that, she'll know I brought her back because I'm a selfish fucking bastard and her strength had me half in love with her the moment I learned she'd killed three vampires. Magical fucking bond aside."

I can still remember that encounter like it was yesterday, standing in the house and having Rainey Astor—a hunter—tell me that the human woman before me managed to kill not one—but three vampires.

It's fucking impressive. Besides, having her level a firearm on me, prepared to defend supernaturals far more powerful than her, was a massive turn-on. Probably shouldn't have been, but it was, and now, here we are.

"She is going through an epic upheaval, brother, give her time."

I sigh. "You're probably right."

"I'm always right." After pushing off the countertop, he claps his hands together. "Now that you're here, how about we go to Eira's place for a drink."

I roll my eyes even as I know I'll be taking him. After losing his ability to dematerialize in the Veil by saving the shifter mate of the eldest Astor sister, I've hung around in case he needed me. Fearghas is the closest thing I've had to a friend since abandoning Faerie centuries ago.

Though I sure as fuck will never admit that to him. The bastard would never let me live it down.

"I guess, though you do realize this borders on stalker."

"And chasing Rachel around for the last few weeks doesn't?"

"Fair point." Reaching out, I clasp a hand on his shoulder and picture where I want to end up. Less than a second later, we're standing in the dining hall of Eira's club. The siren notices us the instant we appear, her violet gaze landing on Fearghas.

"Fuck, she's gorgeous," he whispers loud enough that only I can hear it.

"I wish you two would just get the hell on with it already," I reply as I slide into the booth. I'm bitter, I know it, but I bloody well have every reason to be when the only one who has managed to capture every bit of my heart wants nothing to do with me.

No other woman has ever driven me as mad as Rachel, and if I were a less pathetic man, I might try to convince myself it's because of her disinterest that I want her so badly.

But I am pathetic.

And I would give anything for her to see me as more than the bastard who forced her into a future she didn't want.

"Well, well, well. It must be my lucky night." The siren slides into the booth beside Fearghas, and I choke on a laugh as he stiffens beside her. They haven't been on the best terms since he begged her not to get involved with the war and she refused.

"That it is," I reply.

"You find Rachel?"

I groan, and Fearghas laughs. "He found her; she dismissed him. Poor Ridley doesn't know what to do when he's refused."

"Oh?"

I glare at Fearghas then shift my attention to Eira. "She's alive, back in Billings, and now I can sleep in peace."

A waitress sashays across the dining hall and sets two glasses of whiskey down. "Anything to eat?"

"No."

"No thanks," Fearghas adds with a flirtatious wink. Eira's eyes snap with power though it's so brief I only noticed it because I'm sitting right across from her. It's bloody frustrating to be on the outside, watching two people who would be perfect for each other deny what they really want.

"Let me know if you need anything," she says as she turns and leaves.

Fearghas lifts his glass and takes a drink.

"Hey, assholes. And Eira."

We all glance up as Rainey and Elijah come to a stop beside the booth. I scoot over as she slides in beside me, and Elijah grabs a chair from a nearby table and sets it at the end of our booth.

"How are you?" Eira questions as Rainey groans and leans back.

"Honestly? Exhausted. I swear if I have to answer one more damn call from a human claiming to have a bloodsucking vampire living next door, I'm going to lose my damned mind."

"But what if there is a vampire living next door?" I question.

Elijah snorts but quickly tries to cover it up with a cough.

Her dark gaze levels on me. "Their reason for believing it? They were out mowing their lawn at dawn."

Fearghas laughs and doesn't even bother trying to hide it.

"I'm in a shoot first mood, fairy boy. Better watch your back."

He isn't bothered at all by her insult and simply raises his glass in a mock cheer. "Anytime. Anywhere, little Astor."

"Let's wait until after the wedding. Delaney would be pissed if you offed Fearghas before then," Elijah adds.

"Wedding? You guys settle on a date, then?" Eira asks, her bright smile evidence of just how excited she is at the news. Me? I couldn't fucking care less right now.

Basically, I'm the Grinch when it comes to affection.

Fuck it all. None of its worth a damn.

"We did. New Year's Day."

I grumble, and Rainey glares in my direction. "Problem?"

"No. New Year's Day. So sweet."

"Don't be an ass just because Rachel handed you yours," she shoots back.

Fearghas chuckles. "Exactly."

"Can you all just leave me the fuck alone?"

"Sure, as soon as you stop being a surly asshole. Sound good?"

"Deal."

"Good. Anyway, we're getting married New Year's Day. Super small ceremony, it's going to be great."

"I have money on you turning into a Bridezilla," Fearghas quips. "So if you could get right on that, that'd be great."

"Nice. But I'm good. No Bridezillaness from me. I want my dress and a Skittle wedding cake, and I'm happy."

"A Skittle wedding cake?" Fearghas looks utterly horrified, which does wonders for my mood. "You have got to be kidding."

"Nope. White cake, white frosting, covered in Skittles."

He turns to Elijah. "And you're okay with this?"

"Anything she wants," he replies easily. "I'm just happy to be getting married."

"You are not having a Skittles wedding cake. That's disgusting."

"Says who?"

"Anyone with a fucking taste bud to their name," he shoots back.

"I think it's adorable," Eira replies. "Adorable and unique."

"Thank you, Eira."

She winks at Rainey. Then her gaze drifts to something over my shoulder, and she stands. "I have some business to attend to. I'll see you guys later. Congratulations." She squeezes Elijah's shoulder before heading out.

"So, what's up your ass?" Rainey asks.

"Don't tell her a damned thing until she changes her mind about that atrocious wedding cake."

Since it will annoy him, I choose to answer her. "I successfully chased Rachel back here to Billings."

Her eyebrows arch. "Oh? How did that go?"

"Not great. But my job is done."

"Done, huh?"

"Done. She wants nothing to do with me on any level, so I just wanted to make sure she made it back here where you lot can keep her safe."

"I don't get the impression that Rachel needs anyone to keep her safe."

"She doesn't think so, but there are people out there

who would make her think otherwise," I reply darkly with a pointed look at Fearghas.

"What is that supposed to mean?" Rainey demands as she sits up straighter in the booth. "One of you assholes better tell me what's going on. I just finished one war. I'd love to know if I've got another fight on my hands."

"Nothing like that." I take a deep breath and down the rest of my whiskey. It burns the back of my throat, the momentary buzz so damn enjoyable I wish like hell it would last. Unfortunately, it's gone as quickly as it arrived. *Damn immortal metabolism.* "As you know, we have a dark fae lurking about."

"Yes. The same one who helped us rescue Tarnley."

Mention of the vampire mated to Rachel's closest friend brings a snapshot of her terrified face back into view. I blink rapidly, trying to clear the memory of watching her bleed out on the floor. Finally, it passes, though the terror remains. "Dark fae want what we have," I explain. "They will stop at nothing to obtain light fae magic."

"But she didn't seem too interested in Fearghas's."

"Because she could sense my power. I would have destroyed her in a heartbeat. Rachel is not prepared. She has absolutely no control over her power. To a dark fae, she's a fucking snack. Should any of them discover her, they won't hesitate to steal her power."

"And what happens if they do?"

"Rachel dies," I deadpan. "For good."

"Then why the fuck didn't we kill the dark bitch when we had a chance?"

"She posed no real threat to us then. Rachel was still human, and other than being a chaotic annoyance, there was no real danger until now."

Rainey groans and covers her face with both hands. "You know, I realize that given the fact I'm a hunter, I need the adrenaline of a fight to keep me immortal. However, I swear, one of these days, it's going to kill me."

Elijah reaches over and rubs a hand over his fiancée's back. "We don't know for a fact she's even still in Billings, right?"

"We don't," Fearghas confirms. "And I've been looking."

That's news to me. "Nothing?"

"Not a trace," he tells us. "Honestly, she likely took off after that succubus den."

"Which means there is no immediate threat to Rachel, right?"

I nod at Rainey. "But she still should know it's a possibility."

"Then why don't you go tell her?" Fearghas questions, his grin making me want to repeatedly ram my fist into his face.

"We're not exactly on speaking terms," I reply.

"Then, I tell you what, I'll tell her for you," Rainey replies. "I need to invite her to my wedding anyway."

"You're inviting her to the wedding?"

She grins at me. "I am. I like her. She's tough and annoys the fuck out of you. Two of my favorite qualities. Ready to go?" she asks Elijah.

He nods and stands, returning the chair to where it was. "We're heading out for a hunt if anyone wants to join."

"I'm in." Fearghas downs his drink.

"Same. I could use the burn-off." I slide out and get to my feet, more than ready for the fight. Anything to get my mind off the beautiful woman who I long to have but will never possess.

CHAPTER THREE

RACHEL

"Hello?" I spin in a circle, scanning the meadow for someone—anyone—but see nothing. The green grass is covered in bright flowers, but as my panic begins to set in, the sky darkens, adding to my fear. Where the hell am I? I was literally just in the—memories rush back.

A gunshot.

Pain.

Blood.

Haunting golden eyes.

It all comes rushing back to me, and the blooming ache in my chest grows substantially as realization dawns.

I died.

"Hello!" I scream it now, terrified of what is happening to me. Taking off at a full-blown sprint, I rush forward, running until my lungs should have burned. If I'd still been alive.

Ahead, a massive house comes into view. Relief floods through my body. Maybe I'm not dead; maybe Ridley transported me here somehow. He was there, wasn't he?

A woman stands out in front of the house, and I offer her a wave. Though, with one look at her, I choose to stay a safe distance away. Huge sores cover her greying skin, and patches of her hair are missing as though they'd been ripped from her scalp. "Are you okay?" I ask her.

A breeze flutters by, and I choke as my lungs fill with the putrid stench of rotting flesh.

"Fine. Waiting."

I look behind me then back to her. Is she crazy? Dying? Both? "Who are you waiting for?"

"Someone. He promised to come get me. Leave this place, now." She glares at me then shifts her gaze back to the horizon.

"I haven't seen anyone."

"He promised he would get me out of here. That he would free me if I gave him the wolf."

"Who promised you?"

"The prince."

"Prince?"

She turns back to me. "Why must you ask so many questions, you insolent beast?"

"I—"

"Rachel."

I whirl. Ridley stands just behind me, eyes full of unshed tears. His shoulders slump, and while he's an arrogant bastard, I can think of nothing else but running for him.

So I do.

I sprint toward him, slamming into his body and wrapping both arms around his waist.

His arms come around me, the embrace making me feel safe and secure despite the fear burning a hole through my chest. "Am I dead?" I ask him.

"Not for long," he replies.

I WAKE WITH A JOLT. Heart hammering, I sit up and attempt to take deep breaths to calm my nerves. *In and out. Rachel, get ahold of yourself. It was just a dream.* Except, it wasn't. Nothing about that was a dream. I can still smell the stench of rotting flesh, see the way the ooze crept from her body.

But worse than all of that is the fact that I can still feel Ridley's arms come around me as though I'm the single most important thing in the world to him.

Desperate for fresh air, I toss the blankets off my legs and push to my feet. The carpet is plush beneath my toes as I make my way to the window. Without paying much attention, I throw it open and am met with a biting cold that can only mean one thing: winter is here.

I'm awestruck by the blanket of snow covering the ground just outside my window.

And yet, even though I love everything about this time of year, the sight of it makes me want to cry. I know I'm being ridiculous, that I owe Ridley a fervent thank you, and still, I hope I never see him again.

Maybe then I can get him out of my damned head.

The doorbell chimes, making me jump. Heart hammering, I press my palm to my aching chest and mutter a curse as I head for the door.

Absolutely ridiculous to be so freaked out over a damned doorbell.

"Who is it?"

"Bronywyn."

Thankful it's not Ridley trying to be normal and knock for once, I pull open the door to the petite blonde standing on the other side. The second our gazes meet, she rushes forward and wraps her arms around me in a move that is completely unlike the witch I've known for years.

She's never been overly known for her warm side, but it seems being openly in love has changed that for her.

"Thank goodness you're back." She releases me, so I shut the door.

"I'm sorry I was gone. I needed time to process."

"I completely understand."

"Coffee?" I ask her, and she nods.

"Please."

I head into the kitchen and fill the water tank. As I'm putting the coffee grounds inside the basket, I glance over to see her staring at me. It takes everything in me to resist reaching up and twirling the white ends of my hair. Another gift given to me from whoever the hell runs the Veil Ridley pulled me out of. "I know, I look different."

"Your power signature," Bronywyn corrects. "It's astounding."

I stiffen. "Is that like a smell?"

Bronywyn snorts, and I turn in time to see her bend over at the waist, nearly choking as she struggles to control her laughter.

"What? Do I stink now?"

"Oh my gosh, no!" she takes a couple of deep breaths and manages to straighten, though the humor is still present in her eyes as she levels her gaze back on me. "It's a feeling, the air around you is charged with magic. Very similar to Ridley and Fearghas's."

I don't immediately respond, just continue prepping the coffee pot. *Power signature?* What the hell does that even mean? What does it do? Can everyone feel it?

After pressing the button on the coffee pot, I turn to face her and lean back against my countertop.

"Are you all right?" she asks softly.

Not seeing a point in lying, I shake my head. "Not even a little bit."

"Talk to me. Tell me what's going through your head."

I chew on my bottom lip, unsure how much I should fess up to. I mean, I trust Bronywyn entirely, but telling a supernatural I don't want to be a supernatural seems harsh. Sighing, I shake my head. "I don't know what I am anymore. I mean, I have my memories, my personality, but there's this whole other side to me now, and I have no clue how I'm supposed to handle it."

"What do you want to do?"

"I died a human, Bronywyn—a normal human with normal desires—and now I'm a freaking fairy!"

She snorts. "Don't let Fearghas or Ridley hear you say that."

"Ugh, and then there's Ridley." Covering my face with both hands, I shake my head.

"What about him?"

"He has literally staked a claim on me. Like those old western movies, 'I see this land. It is mine. I'll shoot anyone who tries to claim it from me.'"

I can tell that Bronywyn is mildly amused with my predicament or, more than likely, my explanation of it, and the fact that she's not offended gives me the strength to continue. "It's like I have literally no choice anymore. I can't get married, have kids, be normal. That was all decided for me when he pulled me from the Veil. And now, on top of that, I can't even choose who I want to sleep with for the rest of my life? How the hell is that fair?"

"I don't think that's true," she says softly. "You are still your own person, coming back as a fae didn't change that, it just made you—different. Like a new hair color."

"A new hair color? Really?"

Bronywyn grins and crosses the floor toward me. As soon as she's close, she reaches up to touch my shoulder, and the sunlight glints off the ring on her finger. "Maybe not a new hair color, but think about all the good you can do now. As a fae, you are immune to all human ailments. No flu, no contagious diseases, you can just help people."

"That's if I still have a job."

"From what I understand, Ridley texted some of your co-workers as you and let them know you were ill and needed your leave of absence pushed out."

"Seriously?" Shouldn't that piss me off? Why the hell do I find it mildly thoughtful that he was watching out for me?

"Take things a day at a time, Rachel. One day at a time," she repeats. "That's really all any of us can do."

"I guess." The coffee pot beeps, letting me know it's finished, so I retrieve two mugs and fill them with steaming liquid. "The dematerializing thing will really save on travel."

"Seriously though, I'm jealous about that one."

I slide her cup toward her and lean on the counter, resting my chin on my hand.

Bronywyn chews on her bottom lip before meeting my gaze.

"What?"

She sighs. "You really should talk to Ridley."

Groaning, I drop my face to the countertop. "Not you, too."

"You didn't see him, Rachel. After you died. I mean, shit, he literally snapped the neck of that councilman the moment he pulled that trigger, and as you were dying, he looked like he wanted to die right alongside you."

"Because his magic decided to have a boner for me."

She shakes her head. "It's more than that. Did you ask him what it cost him to pull you out?"

"What do you mean?"

Her eyes narrow on my face as though she's expecting me to already know the answer to my own question. "A fae cannot just go into the Veil and pull someone out. It takes something from them in return. Hell, it can cost them their soul if it chooses to."

My jaw drops as I process what she's said. All of that is news to me, and it certainly puts things into a new perspective. Ridley risked his soul to pull me out? Is the bond on his side really that strong? "I didn't know that."

"That's why Fearghas can't dematerialize. He pulled Cole from the Veil for Delaney."

"Seriously?"

She nods. "Delaney was tricked into killing him, and it destroyed her, so he risked everything to bring him back."

"Shit. You guys have complicated lives."

"That's an understatement." She takes another drink of coffee. "But I really do think you should at least talk to Ridley. You don't want a relationship with him? Fine. But he deserves at least one conversation. The guy did save your life, and if you truly want my opinion on the whole not getting to choose thing? You didn't choose death, right?"

I sigh in defeat because I know I'm being a stubborn ass. "True."

"And are you really mad at Ridley for bringing you back?"

Swallowing hard, I consider her words. I'd told him I wished he would have just left me dead, but honestly, I don't truly believe that. I wish I was still human, sure, but at least, I'm not rotting alongside that creature in the Veil. "Fine. I'll talk to him."

"Good."

Ridley's handsome face swims into view. His grin, the way his eyes blaze with power when he's pissed, it's all I can think about it.

My stomach drops, somersaulting as the world around me disappears. When my feet touch the ground again, I'm standing in what appears to be the living room of an apartment I don't recognize. "What the—"

I turn slowly, studying the masculine space, including a massive lack of personal photographs. In fact, it looks like a staged apartment rather than somewhere someone lives.

The ink on my skin begins to warm, awareness spreading through me which can only mean one thing.

And then he comes around the corner, and I'm struck stupid by the naked chest covered—and I mean *covered* in ink.

"What the hell are you doing here?"

"I—" Ridley steals the very words from my mouth as I continue to gape at him. Green towel hung low on his waist, his bare chest is on full display, and I absolutely devour the intricate tattoos covering his muscled torso. The ink snaking up his forearms and both biceps matches the ink on my own arms, but the rest of it—it's completely unique.

As is the huge scar running down his left pec. I'm drawn to him, a moth to a flame, and before I know it, I'm taking a cautious step toward him.

He, however, remains rooted in his spot. "What are you doing here, Rachel?"

His sharp tone rips me from my stupor. "I wanted to talk to you."

Eyebrows drawn together, he glares as he crosses both muscled arms over his chest. "And your phone was broken?"

"Look, I don't know how any of this demateriaizing crap works yet. I thought about talking to you, and here I am."

"Then think about being somewhere else," he replies as he turns on his heel and stalks away.

I follow. I shouldn't, I know, but his complete disinterest in talking to me pisses me off. "Hey, I'm not done!"

"I am. And unless you want to see me naked, I suggest you turn around and walk away."

The urge to remain where I am while he drops that towel is strong, but to save myself some serious drooling, I decide to do exactly what he suggested. Well, almost what he suggested. Instead of leaving, I head into the living room and plop down onto his couch.

I'm not so arrogant to believe my minor interactions with the supernaturals Bronywyn brought me over the years were enough to teach me everything I need to know. This whole world is brand new to me. I know my immediate reaction has less to do with *what* I am now and more to do with the simple fact that I've had enough decisions made for me over the years, that the idea I have lost complete control over my own destiny is smothering.

I have to have control.

But that control can't come at the expense of me being a bitch to the one person who literally risked his soul to save me. Even if I know, deep down, I can't give him what he actually wants from me: my heart.

CHAPTER FOUR

RIDLEY

loody damned women. Why the hell can't she just leave me be? She sure as hell expected me to leave her alone, didn't she?

And now, even though I asked her to leave, I can feel her out there, the ink on my arms reacting to her nearness. It's a soul bond I've heard very little about and one I *never* wanted to experience.

I tug on some sweats and a t-shirt then head out into my living room where she waits, her gorgeous body looking entirely too fucking delicious on the dark cushions of my couch.

"Still here, then? Who's stalking who now?" I head into the kitchen and purposely only retrieve one bottle of water. Then I return to the living room and sit down on the opposite side of my sectional.

"You've decided to stick with the whole asshole thing, then?"

"Why change what works? What the hell do you want, Rachel? You made it pretty damned clear you want nothing to do with me."

"That was before—" she starts but trails off, closing her eyes tightly as though she's struggling to form the words.

Her beauty—never in my life have I ever met a woman who pulls at every part of me. Her beauty, strength, shit—the proverbial balls on this woman—she's the complete package, and it takes all of my self-restraint not to slide to my knees and beg her to give me a chance.

That's not who I am, though. I do not beg. I *will* not beg.

"Before what?"

Her eyes open, and I suck in a breath. The connection between us is as volatile as dynamite, that's for damn sure. "Bronywyn told me that you had to pay a price to bring me back."

Fucking witches. Always meddling where they shouldn't be. "I did."

"What was it?"

"You're not stupid."

Her cheeks flush red, and I wish I could go back and say it again just to watch the color show for the first time. "No. I'm not. But I don't know enough about this —" She gestures between us. "—to be able to answer that question for myself."

I know she's right, but on top of being arrogant, I'm sadistic as fuck, and seeing her pissed off at me is easier than the look of pity she was giving me a moment ago. "The Veil took a piece of my soul," I explain, not bothering to pull punches. Better she knows exactly what she's getting into.

Rachel's mouth falls slack and she gapes at me. "Your soul?"

"Yes. And to compensate, they linked us together. Permanently. For me, anyway. I'm pretty sure you can still do whatever the hell you want."

"The ink." She gestures to the tattoos on her creamy skin and then to the ones on my arms.

"Yes. We are soul-marked. Your soul recognizes mine because it's literally what's keeping me alive."

"Wait a damned minute." She shuts her eyes tightly and shakes her head. "Keeping you alive like Bronywyn's link to Tarnley?"

"Exactly like that. Though, our bond cannot be broken with a redirect spell." Because I'm so damned uncomfortable with the fact that I am practically telling her she owns me, I push to my feet. "Water?"

"Sure. Thanks." She remains silent, sitting on my

couch as she stares blankly ahead at the fireplace in the corner.

Shock? Awe? I'm pretty sure my revelation brought both to the table.

After grabbing another bottle of water, I turn and head back to the living room and offer it to her. I try not to hate the fact that she doesn't look at me when she takes it.

Minutes tick by in complete silence. Every part of me yearns to close the distance between us and show her just how good we can be, but I don't dare move. I may be an asshole, but I know the changes she's facing right now require some massive processing.

"So I was right then?" She whispers it, the words barely audible.

"About what?"

When she turns toward me and I see the unshed tears in her eyes, I want to rip my own heart out and offer it to her on a silver fucking platter. Hers to keep, hers to destroy. "I lost all choice in my future. I have no control over anything. Again." Rachel covers her face with both hands as her shoulders shake.

Because I literally—even after however the fuck long I've been alive—I still cannot tolerate a woman crying, I let go of my pride and kneel before her. "You lost control of nothing," I promise.

"I did. We're tied to each other, Ridley. Permanently. Forever."

"No."

She looks up at me now, eyes glistening.

"I am tied to you," I confirm. "Not the other way around."

"That means—"

"It means nothing. I'm fine. Just don't die, and neither will I." Hoping it will calm her down, I flash a smile, but because I can't help myself, I also reach up and tuck stray strands of hair behind her ears.

She freezes at my touch, mouth falling slack, gaze bearing straight through me. "I don't know you."

"I know that."

"And to be honest, your first impression sucked."

"Well, since we're being honest, you caught me off guard," I tell her. "Never, in a million years, did I think my magic would bond with anyone, especially not some puny human." I grin again, hoping she'll recognize the joke in my words.

And thankfully, she does. "Well, I didn't ever think I'd cross paths with an arrogant fairy bastard, so I guess we were both wrong."

"Again, not a fairy. As I said, note the lack of glitter."

"And I was not a puny human. Note the ability to drop three vampires." She returns my smile, though it doesn't reach her eyes. Then, finally, she takes a deep breath. "Okay. Enough pity party for me. I am what I am now, and I am grateful that you brought me back."

The lump in my throat grows substantially. "You're welcome."

"So I'm a fae."

"Yes."

"Can you teach me what I can do?"

Her innocence in that moment, her openness, it soothes a part of me I hadn't realized was damaged. "Absolutely."

The joy in her smile is blinding. She holds out a hand. "Friends?"

I take it instantly, knowing it might be the only contact I get from her, while also realizing being nothing more than her friend will likely torture me until the end of time. "Friends." Our gazes hold, and my heart hammers in my chest. This physical reaction, it's new to me. Sure, I've lusted before, hell, I've even loved. Lucy was the closest I came—before I realized how crazy she was—to having genuine affection for anyone but Flora.

What I feel for Rachel, though, it surpasses anything I have ever felt for anyone else. "When do you have to go back to work?" I ask as I pull my hand back.

"I don't actually know. Thanks for telling them I was sick, by the way."

"You're welcome. I had to glamour myself and answer a Facetime call, by the way."

She blinks rapidly. "You did what?"

"Serena Facetimed you, and I answered it—as you. A few days before I found you in New York. I just wanted to make sure you knew in case she said something."

She looks genuinely stunned, and it's so damned

adorable I have to get up off the floor and put some distance between us. "Thanks," she says.

"You're welcome."

"Hey, Ridley?"

I turn back toward her. "What?"

"Where is Faerie?"

I smile, feeling like finally, my life might actually start making sense. "I'll show it to you when you're ready." *When you care for me as much as I do you, I'll take you there and show you where I come from, mate.*

———

THE MOMENT the world around me comes into view, I grin wildly at Fearghas. He offers me a nod then continues sipping coffee in the booth he frequents at Eira's. It's ridiculous, the amount of time he spends here, but I get it now.

Because I want to be around Rachel all the damned time, even if she only wants to see me occasionally.

"What has you all chipper this morning?" he asks as I slide into the booth across from him.

"Rachel and I had a nice chat."

"Oh?"

"I'm going to train her to use her abilities."

"Nice."

"I think it will be, and it will give my master plan time to work."

"What master plan is that?"

"I am going to make her fall in love with me."

That gets his attention. He sits up straighter and grips his coffee mug. "Fall in love with you? Really? That's your big plan?"

"It is. Unlike you, I don't want to spend eternity alone."

"And you think I do? Shit, I'm trying over here."

"Your subtly is an art, my friend. But it's not going to get the girl."

"Subtle? Really? My intentions couldn't be more apparent if I hired an orchestra and sung my feelings to Eira."

I snort, the mental image bringing me a shit ton of joy. "That would be a sight."

"One day," he says wistfully. "When the time is right, she'll see."

To be honest, I'm not an overly soft person. But seeing the pain in my friend's eyes, it hurts me a bit. Of course, I won't fucking admit it to anyone. The last thing I need is people discovering I have actual real feelings about shit. Then they'll want to talk about them, and it will be a whole big snowball effect I'd much rather avoid.

"I agree with you," I tell him. "Now. Where should I start with Rachel?"

"You're coming to me to ask for advice? Really?"

"Who the hell else am I going to ask?"

He stares at me for a moment. "Literally anyone

else. Rainey, Delaney, Elijah, Cole, Tarnley, Bronywyn —they all have better track records."

"Perhaps. But you're the only other fae around. You know as well as I do things are a bit different for us."

"I guess."

We fall into companionable silence as Fearghas stares blankly ahead. I know he's looking for her, searching for the one who his magic has claimed. "By the way, have you told anyone?"

"Fuck, no," he replies, knowing exactly what I'm referring to. "That's the last damn thing I need getting out. Everyone already looks at me like I'm a sad puppy begging for scraps."

"I mean—if the shoe fits."

He glares at me. "You want my help, don't you?"

"I do."

"Good. Ask Bronywyn."

"That's your advice?"

"She knows Rachel better than anyone. You want to win the doctor over? I'd start with her friends."

"Good point." I clap my hands together. "Isn't this exciting? I've never done this before."

"What?"

"Tried to woo a woman. It always just happened naturally."

Fearghas rolls his eyes. "You might want to turn that shit down before I lose my breakfast all over this table."

I grin at him. "Don't be jealous, brother. Your time will come."

"Sometimes, I very much doubt that," he adds with a sigh as Eira walks out from the back. Their gazes meet, and for a heartbeat, I feel like an obtrusive third wheel.

But seconds later, she's turning away, and Fearghas is redirecting his attention on the coffee mug in front of him.

Chapter Five

Rachel

Walking into the hospital does more for my morale than anything else has over the last few weeks. I seriously cannot even begin to hide the smile on my face. Dressed in navy blue scrubs, I finally feel like myself again.

My normal, human, doctor self.

"Rachel!" Serena rushes out and wraps her arms around me in a heavy hug. "How are you?"

Returning the hug, I take the extra time to let myself sink into the simplicity of the embrace. No destiny, no soul mate, no fae abilities—just me and my friend. When I release her, I smile widely. "I'm okay, just needed some time."

Her face falls, and I know she's thinking back to the humans murdered the night the vampires came for Detective Walker Alan, Rainey's partner. "I can't even imagine what you must have felt."

My throat tightens. There'd been so much blood. So much death. And for a brief moment, I'm transported back to that bathroom, hiding with my gun as I try to remain as quiet as possible while waiting for backup to arrive.

Yet another reason to be grateful for my abilities because now I can be that backup. I stand a little straighter, picturing how differently that night could have gone had I been what I am now. "All is okay now. I'm back. What did I miss?"

"The police wrapped up their investigation. A gas leak sent one of the patients into a craze. It is so insane to me, but it could have been so much worse. Could you imagine if more had been affected that way?"

My stomach churns at the lie told to keep the supernaturals at bay. As of now, I am the only one here who knows the truth. I killed three of them, and Rainey finished off the fourth right before Tarnley, Bronwyn's vampire mate, ripped their heads off and brought his cleaners in to erase the evidence of the supernatural attack.

It was a long, depressing night.

"Rachel?"

I turn as the hospital's Chief of Medicine, Dr. Dollins calls my name. "Yes?"

"I'd like to speak with you in my office."

My stomach drops, mind instantly going to worst-case scenario. But then I remember that I can tell him the truth. He may not believe me, but since supernaturals have been outed now, I can at least give him a minor summary of where I've been for the past few weeks.

"Good luck," Serena whispers as I turn away and follow Dr. Dollins to his office at the end of the hall.

"Close the door."

I do as he says and take a seat in one of the leather-backed chairs across from his desk. He's silent a moment, not meeting my eye.

"Am I in trouble? I'm sorry I was out, I was—"

"I know where you were. Detectives Astor and Alan came by yesterday and explained to me that you were helping them with medical assistance after the war. That your leave of absence was necessary to protect you from the press or anyone who might want to harm those who assisted them."

Well, that's news. "Really? I mean, yes, yes I was, I'm just surprised they came in."

"It was a huge upheaval for our city for the supernaturals to be outed, but I'm grateful that you are close with the detective and that you helped."

"I am."

He sighs. And when he does meet my eye, something shifts in the air around us. It's subtle and completely new to me. "I assume she's told you what I am."

I stiffen in my seat, noting his slumped shoulders and the nervous way he's fondling the pen in his hands. "Yes?" it comes out as a question, though I didn't mean it too.

"I trust we can keep that between us, right? I don't want any trouble, and I've worked hard to maintain secrecy in my life."

"Of course, sir. I won't say anything."

His visible relief is enough to have me bookmarking that question for Rainey later. What the hell is he?

"Good, thank you. I also wanted to tell you how sorry I am that I wasn't here to help when those vampires attacked. Detective Astor explained to me that you put three of them down to protect her partner."

"I did."

"That took balls, Rachel. You are an impressive woman." He flashes a smile at me, and if I'm not mistaken, it bordered on mild attraction.

"I didn't want them to hurt my patient."

"You knew what they were? Before they attacked?"

I nod.

"And you didn't run." He runs a hand through his

thick brown hair. "Impressive woman indeed." He stands. "If you need anything, please let me know."

I follow suit and get to my feet. "I will, Dr. Dollins, thank you."

"Just Max, please."

"Max." Saying his first name feels strange, but not nearly as strange as the attraction I sense coming from him.

"It really is good to have you back, Rachel."

"It's good to be back, thanks." Heat rushes to my cheeks as he maintains eye contact, and finally, I force myself to look away. I've always thought he was attractive, young for the position even, but now I get it. The guy is a supernatural.

Apparently, I was closer to them than I thought.

AFTER A TWELVE-HOUR SHIFT, my feet are exhausted, but I cannot recall a time I felt better than I do right now. I walk out of the hospital and into the chilly December air, wearing a smile on my face.

And then I see *him*. Leaned up against the hood of my car is Ridley dressed in dark jeans and an olive sweatshirt. My heart does a somersault in my chest as my palms grow sweaty, nerves and attraction battling for the number one spot in my mind.

Just friends, I remind myself. Who the hell knows

how long that will last, but for now, being just friends alleviates a lot of pressure. "Hey, what are you doing here?"

"Figured we could get started on your training," he replies as he pushes off of my car. "How was your day? Asking as a friend," he adds quickly. "Friends can ask about friends' days can't they?"

"They can," I reply, slightly concerned he may have a screw loose. What changed? "It was good. Felt great to be back."

He beams at me. "Good. Now, let's grab some food, and then we'll start."

"Food?"

"Take out. I'm craving some *Taco Bell*."

"*Taco Bell*," I repeat.

"You doing okay, Rachel? Or is it typical for you to repeat everything?"

"No, I just didn't think anyone ever craved *Taco Bell*."

"Well," he says, "I do, and I would love to grab something to eat before we get started."

I unlock my car, and he climbs into the passenger seat as I toss my backpack into the back before sliding behind the wheel. The moment the door closes, I'm assaulted with the masculine scent that is Ridley. Pine and leather, a potent combination that somehow manages to weaken my knees, making me damn grateful I'm already sitting down.

"How was your day?" I ask, needing to fill the silence with anything to distract me from picturing him in nothing but a towel.

"Uneventful," he replies easily. "Had some coffee with Fearghas then spent the afternoon helping Rainey sort through multiple complaints from humans."

"Helping her sort through? What do you mean?"

"She had me go check out about half a dozen possible supernaturals; they weren't, just humans who'd pissed off their neighbors or coworkers."

"And you helped her?"

"Sure. I like Rainey."

I don't know why—certainly doesn't make any sense at all—but that simple fact leaves me with a bout of jealousy. "That's cool."

"You know, she and Elijah are getting married on New Year's Day."

Jealousy gone. "Really? I didn't know they set a date."

"Found out yesterday. She's going to invite you."

I chuckle. "Thanks for the heads up."

"Anytime, friend."

I guide my car into the drive-thru line of *Taco Bell*, stopping just behind a white SUV. "Where are we starting?"

"Training?"

I nod.

"I figure we should work on you controlling your

dematerializing abilities. You know, can't have you popping in when I'm naked anymore." He winks, and heat rushes to my cheeks as that image I was working hard to block slams into my memory.

Heat pools between my legs, the warmth spreading from my arm tattoos through my body. *Damn delicious fae.* My promise to myself has literally never been more frustrating, but I made it for a reason, and that reason is what cools my jets. "I appreciate that. It seems so random. Like, I'll think about Bronywyn or Rainey, but I don't ever end up materializing in front of them."

He nods in understanding as we pull forward a bit. "Likely it's our connection that has something to do with that. The fact that I'm soul-bound to you would make things a bit more complicated. With dematerializing, you have to be able to pinpoint where you want to go; then you focus your magic on that. A Dorothy back to Kansas type of scenario."

I gape at him. "Did you seriously just quote The Wizard of Oz?"

"I did. Apparently, it's Bronywyn's favorite movie. I stopped by to see her and Tarnley for a bit this afternoon and ended up sitting through it."

Snorting, I shake my head. "I learn a little bit more about you every day."

"That's the whole point to friendship, isn't it?"

I glance over at him, and our gazes hold. My body is so warm around him, my thoughts so muddled, it's near impossible to decide what is real and what is magic.

Maybe there is no difference.

There has to be.

The car in front of me moves, so I pull forward to the box.

"Hello, welcome to *Taco Bell*. Order when ready."

Chapter Six

RIDLEY

I'd spent quite a bit of time in Rachel's apartment when I was searching for clues as to where to find her. But standing here when she's showering less than twenty feet away is doing things to me I really would rather not focus on.

Naked.

Soapy.

Wet.

I adjust myself, my cock preparing for something that is not happening. *Get it the fuck together, Ridley.*

I briefly considered heading to Faerie for a few hours, but that could very well turn into days, and not seeing her for that long would drive me mad at this point.

The water shuts off, so I move further away from the bathroom door and focus every bit of attention I have on the photographs lining her walls. I'm especially drawn to the images of her when she'd been overseas with Doctors Without Borders, something I learned from Bronywyn that afternoon when I'd stopped by to see her.

Such an intriguing woman, Rachel is, and I cannot wait to learn more.

The door opens, and she steps out, face naked, hair soaking wet, wearing leggings and a baggy t-shirt. My mouth goes dry, my body urging me to move forward, to claim her, to show her how good we can be together.

I take a step forward.

Rachel clears her throat. "Thanks for waiting. I really needed to wash the day off of me."

Sensing her nervousness, I nod. "No problem."

"Let me grab my shoes, and we can get going."

She crosses the floor to the hall closet and starts to bend over, so I force myself to turn around. No need for additional torture by getting a full view of her perfect ass. "I want to start by showing you how to do it, then we'll have you try. Deal?"

"Sounds great." I sense her growing closer, a warmth climbing up my spine and settling throughout my body. Turning I face her and get a whiff of the delicate lavender of what I'm assuming is either body wash or lotion.

Frankly, the mental image of her applying either is too damn much for me to deal with. "Can I have your hands?" Something dark flickers across her expression. "I need to be touching you to dematerialize with you."

"Oh, yeah. Sorry."

I long to ask her what happened, why she's so hesitant, but I also get the impression that Rachel is private, and the last thing I want to do is push her. Not when I am playing the long game here. Her slender hands slip into mine, and I shiver, a violent tremor rushing through my body at the contact.

When her eyes widen, her lips parting slightly, I know she feels it too.

I clear my throat. "As I mentioned before, dematerializing takes a good amount of focus, and you have to have a mental image of where you are going."

She snorts. "That explains why I ended up deep in the Manhattan River and nearly drowned."

My fingers tighten on hers. "What? When?"

"When I went there. I just wanted to go to New York, and I pictured the city and the river, and that's where I ended up. I panicked until I realized I could get out of it easy enough."

"Once, I materialized in front of a car on a dark highway and nearly ended up pavement decoration."

"Are you serious?"

"Yep. The driver was half asleep, but I was undoubtedly a deer in the headlights. It was an awkward conversation for sure because I'd been so shocked I hadn't been able to dematerialize for a good twenty-four hours."

Her laughter is so fucking welcome I want to do anything and everything to hear it over and over again for the rest of my immortal life. "I'm glad I'm not alone."

"You're not, I assure you. Where do you want to go?"

"I have to have been there before?"

"You do right now, yes. But when you get a bit more practiced, a general location—preferably with a picture —makes the transport easier. Though, I can now picture a basic living space, plus the person I want to see, and end up in the living room of damn near anyone's home."

"That is so cool."

"Eh, they always seem less happy about it."

Rachel chuckles then bites down on her bottom lip. She captures it between her teeth, torturing me in the process. My blood hammers through my veins, my heart about to beat the fuck right out of my chest. And my cock—well—let's just fucking hope she doesn't look down.

That would get awkward.

"I honestly don't know. Surprise me?"

"Oh, Rachel, I'm full of surprises." I wink and then

picture where I want to go, and the world around us disappears. Moments later, we're standing on the top of a cliff in one of my favorite places in the world.

"Oh my gosh," she whispers. She keeps hold of one of my hands but releases the other. I pretend not to notice as we both turn to stare out at an impossibly blue ocean bathed in shades of red and gold from the receding sun.

"Santorini, Greece."

"It's magnificent."

"I come here a lot. It's one of my favorite places."

She shifts her attention to me. "Seriously?"

"It's gorgeous, the perfect place to think." As cheesy as it is, I want to tell her it's even more beautiful now that she's here, but I keep that particular truth to myself. I know that our bond is what's driving a good portion of my case of insta-love, but I can't be bothered to care.

This woman, she is exactly what I've been looking for.

I just didn't know it.

"Come with me." Still holding her hand, I pull her toward a path that will lead us into town.

"Where are we going?"

"You'll see." We head down the path, and the lights in the village just ahead illuminate our way as I guide Rachel toward one of my oldest friends and the only human who knew of my existence until—well—I ran into the Astor sisters.

As we walk, I glance at Rachel, happy to see she is taking everything in. "This is—I never thought I'd make it here."

"Dematerializing has its perks."

"No damned joke. This is, it's incredible."

The faded sign for my friend's restaurant comes into view, and I can't help my smile. I used to get over here weekly, but with everything going on over the past few months—supernatural war and all—it's been nearly six months since I've seen—Aleixo!" I greet with a wide smile as he steps out of his restaurant.

He throws up both hands. "Ridley! My friend! Where have you been?"

"Busy."

Aleixo's dark eyes drift to Rachel, and he smiles knowingly. "I see that." He rushes forward and snatches her free hand and presses a kiss to the top. "Who might this lovely lady be?"

"Rachel," she replies easily. "So nice to meet you, Aleixo."

"You too. Ridley has never brought a woman here before."

Rachel turns to me, and I fight the embarrassment I'm sure she can see all over my face. I reach back with my free hand and rub the back of my neck. "Yeah, well, I don't date much."

"Nonsense. Young man like you? I imagine you date plenty. Come, come, let me feed you." He ushers us inside and over to a table near the window. "Be right back with your usual plus one." He winks at Rachel then disappears into the back.

"So, come here often?"

I snort at her cheesy line. "Once a week since he opened the place in 1967."

"1967? Seriously? That would make him—"

"Seventy-two, but don't mention it. He's a bit testy about his age."

"He doesn't look any older than mid-fifties!" She looks stunned. Honestly, it's adorable.

"Aleixo claims it's all the sun and fresh air."

"Well, whatever it is, it's working." She's quiet for a moment, her gaze drifting out the window. I take her distraction and study her profile, the shape of her nose, her jaw. How a woman like this is still single is a mystery to me. "Wait, you've been coming here since 1967?"

"Yes."

"Hasn't he noticed that—" She stops speaking and looks around at the otherwise empty dining room then leans in closer. "—you haven't changed?"

I take the opportunity to lean in close and whisper, "He knows I'm a fae."

She pales, the color leaving her cheeks for a nanosecond, and I can do nothing but stare like a bloody teenager meeting his wet dream for the first time.

"How?"

Because it's the safest possible option for both of us,

I pull away and sit firmly in my chair. "As I said, I'm pretty sure he's a supernatural. But, that aside, he guessed it after I materialized in front of him on a highway and he nearly hit me."

"That's deer-in-the-headlights-guy?"

I chuckle. "It is."

Her brows draw together in confusion, and it's the most adorable thing I've ever seen. "Can't you guys memory wipe?"

"We can, and I definitely considered it. But after talking with the guy for a bit and having him try to calm me down with food after I appeared out of thin air in front of him, I decided it was nice to have someone to talk to. And, well, here we are." I lift both hands, gesturing to the inside of the tiny café.

Just then, Aleixo rushes forward with a tray boasting two of the most gorgeous Greek salads I have ever seen. "We will start off with these, and I have to gyros coming your way."

"Thank you."

"You are most welcome, my friend." He leaves me there, something that is not typical for him since he usually sits with me while I eat. My guess is he's doing it to give me some alone time with the woman across from me.

"This looks fantastic."

"It's amazing. The vegetables are fresh, crispy, and the feta cheese—it's to die for." I slide my fork down into the slab of feta over the top. It's one of my favorite things about Greek salads in Greece—they don't crumble the feta on top. It's left solid on top and covered in aromatic, delicious spices.

We both take our bites at the same time, and I damn near groan with pleasure. One of my favorite things about being immortal? The food. It's one of the true pleasures of life, and humans tend to get so wrapped up in their lives and fad diets that they rarely take the time to enjoy what it means to truly live.

"This is even better than I imagined!" she exclaims as soon as she's swallowed the first bite.

I grin at her. "Stick with me, and I'll show you all the good food. Let me tell you, you haven't truly lived until you've eaten authentic Texas barbeque."

Her laughter fills my ears, and for the briefest of moments, I let myself fall into the idea that this could be my new forever.

Unfortunately for me, I also know that beautiful moments like this? They rarely last.

CHAPTER SEVEN

RACHEL

With a basket of freshly baked blueberry muffins in hand, I step into the Billings police department. All around me, people are answering phone call after phone call, each one of them looking even more exasperated than the last. The desks are all empty while the phones at the receptionist area are ringing off the hook. It's pure chaos.

While this is my first time in a police station, I can honestly say it's nothing like I pictured it. Aren't detectives supposed to be sitting at their desks? Going over evidence and researching suspects? Or does it only happen that way in the movies?

"Rachel?"

I glance over at the familiar voice and smile widely as Detective Walker Alan stalks toward me. Dressed in jeans and a black t-shirt, his shoulder holster situated across his broad shoulders, he looks every bit the homicide detective he is and, thankfully, nothing like the man who was wheeled into my hospital on his death bed what now feels like lifetimes go. "Hey! How are you feeling?"

He leans down and offers me a hug that I graciously accept. "So much better. Damn near back at my fighting weight."

"Good. I'm so glad. Rainey started letting you out yet?"

He snorts. "Not a damned chance. She says another week, but we'll see. Come on, I'll take you to her."

"Thanks." I fall into step beside him. "Is it always this crazy?"

"Hardly. People are calling for everything from sneezes to minor traffic altercations, claiming supernaturals are out of control. Rainey is going to snap one of these days and pump the phones full of bullets."

Unable to help myself, I bark out a laugh. Mainly because I can absolutely see that happening.

Walker guides me through a door where Rainey sits

at a desk, fingers pressed to her temples. "What is that delicious smell?" she asks the moment we step inside.

"Blueberry muffins," I reply easily.

She grins at me. "You are absolutely my favorite person right now." Getting up from her chair, she rushes over to me as I pull back the cloth covering and offer her a muffin from the basket. While it's open, Walker grabs one too.

"Walker said things are pretty wild around here."

"That's an understatement. You know, I'm prepared to get fired for claiming it was nothing but a publicity stunt."

"It's definitely impossible to stash the cat back in the bag."

"I'm going to find a way because this is outrageous."

"It'll calm down," Walker adds. "Soon."

"I sure as fuck hope so because I can't walk into a damned grocery store to get Skittles without being glamoured these days. The moment I do, it's like a fucking stampede." She plops back down in her chair and props both booted feet up on the corner of her desk. "Oh, what are you doing on January first?" she asks, popping some muffin into her mouth."

"Nothing that I'm aware of."

"Wanna come to a wedding?"

My smile is instant. "I would love that."

"Great. I'll get you more details as we get them."

"You excited?"

"Definitely. I've never been one who wanted a huge

wedding, shit, I never wanted to get married at all, so it will be intimate. Being married to Elijah, though, I honestly cannot wait for that." Her bright smile portrays so much love, so much joy, that my heart yearns for even a fraction of that happiness. "Speaking of, how are things with Ridley?"

Yearning gone. "What do you mean?"

"I assume you've realized he's super into you, right?"

"He's made that clear, but it's just the magic. For some reason, he was bonded to me even before the whole soul-bound thing happened."

"Soul bound?" Interest piqued, Walker props a hip on the free corner of Rainey's desk.

"Apparently, when he pulled me out of the Veil, it cost him a part of his soul. To compensate, whoever took it, in the first place, bound him to me." I set the basket down on the desk and pull up the sleeves of my sweatshirt, showcasing the black ink trailing up my arms in intricate swirls.

"Damn. That's big." Walker runs a hand over the back of his hair. "Did you know?" he asks Rainey.

"Nope, though, to be honest, I've had my hands full." Her eyes remain on my tattoos though.

"He's—" I search for a word. "Different. I don't want to just be a solution to his problem, though," I admit honestly.

"You think that's what he's after?" Rainey asks.

I shrug. "I don't know, but I do know I've been on

74

the opposite side of plenty of arrogant bastards, and it never works out."

"Ridley may be an arrogant bastard, but he's a good man. When we needed help, he stuck around."

"That's true." And probably the only reason I agreed to be friends. Because I have seen the side of him that wasn't bossing me around and telling me what to do.

"Maybe it's because I'm engaged, but I say see where the feelings take you."

"Rainey Astor. You big softy, you," Walker jokes.

She glares up at him. "Watch it. I'm still prone to violent outbursts." The detective turns her dark gaze my way. "That why you come by today? Or was there something else?"

"Something else. My boss pulled me into his office yesterday and told me that he wanted to make sure his 'secret' was safe with me? That you knew what it was, and I guess he assumed you told me?"

She snorts. "He's a super. A rogue feline shifter."

"Rogue?"

"Has no pack," Walker replies. "On his own, it's not unusual for feline shifters to run alone, but to have one so high up in a hospital is a surprise. It's impressive he got the certifications to make him legitimate."

"Which he did. I checked," Rainey adds. "If he's a fraud, he's a good one."

"Interesting."

"You didn't tell him what you are, right?" she asks, and I shake my head.

"Didn't seem relevant."

"Good. From what I understand, you need to keep that under wraps."

"Why?"

"You heard we had a dark fae in Billings?"

"The one that pretended to be Bronywyn's mom?"

"One and the same. Anyway, according to Fearghas and Ridley, they seek out weak light fae so they can steal their magic."

"Weak?"

"Inexperienced would be a better word for it," Walker injects. "You're new to your power, which makes you particularly vulnerable."

"Why the hell didn't he tell me this last night?"

"Last night? You guys were together last night?" Rainey asks right before she shakes her head. "Forget it, none of my business. Shit, I've been hanging around with Fearghas way too much lately. It's making me a gossip."

Walker snorts.

Meanwhile, I'm far too freaked out to find humor in anything. It is one thing to have my life altered forever, but now I'm a target? Hunted by a dark fae who managed to kill a succubus queen with nothing more than a hand gesture? What the hell does that mean for me?

"If it makes you feel any better, Fearghas has been out hunting her. He says he's seen no trace of her at all and that she more than likely took off after their altercation."

"She literally tried to make you and Bronywyn tear each other apart," I remind her. "I'll be a sitting duck until I learn about what I am."

"Guess it's a good thing you're spending time with Ridley then. According to Fearghas, he's old as fuck."

"I'm not super thrilled he kept this from me," I tell her. "In fact, it pisses me the hell off. We were together for hours last night while we were working on my demateri-alizing control. He should have—" The ground disappears beneath my feet, and before I know it, I'm standing on a dance floor full of gyrating bodies. A hot body presses up against my back seconds before breath fans over my neck.

"Hey there, gorgeous, what are you doing here?" Firm hands go to my hips, gripping me and yanking me back against him as he grinds into me.

"I—I think I made a mistake." I try to pull away, but he rips me back against him. The strobe light overhead makes it impossible to see anything but the gyrating bodies surrounding me.

I panic, my body seizing. I don't know where I am, who I'm with—why the hell can't I leave?

"I think you're in the right spot, pretty. Tell you what, why don't you just bend over for a second." A hand slips up my back and tries to shove me forward.

I try to pull away, but he bands me back. "Playing hard to get, huh? I can work with that."

"Get your fucking hands off her now before I relieve you of them," a familiar voice snarls.

"Easy, man, not looking for any trouble." The hands disappear from my waist, and I breathe a sigh of relief as another closes over my arm.

"What the hell are you doing?"

I whirl on Ridley. His eyes, typically calm, are glowing with power as he glares down at me like I'm the one who fucked up. "What am *I* doing? Really? That's what you have the balls to ask me right now?" I rip my arm from his grasp. "What the fuck are you doing? And why didn't you tell me someone might be hunting me?"

He looks around, gaze traveling over the bodies around us all moving together. Did I freaking materialize in the center of an orgy? I focus on Ridley now, looking for any signs he'd been partaking, but he's fully dressed, wearing dark jeans and a *Gaming Nerd* t-shirt. "Come with me."

I let him tug me off the dance floor because, to be honest, I'm pretty sure some of these people are having public sex, and while I'm no prude, the last thing I want to do is bump into a stranger as they're getting their rocks off.

We move off the floor, and the second we're away from the dancing, all loud music disappears. "What the —" I turn toward the dance floor, expecting not to see it, but it's still there. Everyone is still moving to the beat of the music even though I can't hear it anymore.

"Magic. Come." Ridley continues pulling me through wherever the hell we are until we enter a dining room where I instantly recognize three of the present parties.

"Rachel! So nice to see you!" Eira greets. The siren effortlessly glides across the floor and comes to a stop in front of me. "You can let her go now, Ridley."

Reluctantly, he releases me, though he doesn't move.

"How did you get here?" Tarnley questions.

"I don't—"

"The bond between us allows her to travel to places she's never been as long as I'm there," Ridley interrupts. "Though, perhaps next time, you should materialize somewhere you won't get air fucked."

That does it. All embarrassment, fear, whatever the hell I was feeling vanishes, and I whirl on him. Finger pointed, I jab it into his chest. "Listen here, asshole, you know good and damn well I have no control over that ability—first off. And secondly, you kept a pretty massive fucking secret from me, so how about you cut the shit!"

"Oh, damn," I hear Fearghas mutter as Eira slides out of view.

Meanwhile, we might as well be the only ones in the room. Ridley reaches up and grabs my shoulder again, and the scenery shifts. Within moments, we're standing in the living room of my apartment.

He releases me. "I'm sorry."

It was so different than what I was expecting that I am caught off guard. Sorry? He's sorry? Do I even have an argument prepared for that? Sunlight streams in through my windows, reminding me that it's mid-morning and I have to be at work soon. "For which part? What the hell were you doing in a sex club anyway?"

The corners of his mouth twitch. "Sex club? I'll be sure to relay your opinion of Eira's establishment to her the next time I see her.

Realization dawns, and I could facepalm myself if I wasn't wanting to avoid further embarrassment. Having a stranger's dick pressed against my ass was enough for one night—or rather day. "That was Eira's club."

"Yes. Supernaturals do get down pretty frequently, and since a lot of them can't go out in the day, being at a club all morning is a pretty common occurrence."

"That makes sense."

"Good. Then it's settled." He crosses his arms. "Now, what secret is it we're talking about?"

"Dark fae? Ring a bell?"

He pales slightly. "Rainey talked to you."

"Because you were too much of a coward!" I shoot back. "Didn't want to interrupt our evening to tell me that there is someone hunting me?"

"She's not hunting you," he replies. "Though if she finds out you're here, that will likely change. We just have to find her first."

"Why didn't you tell me?"

"And risk worrying you before there was anything to worry about?" He shakes his head. "You've got enough on your plate, and frankly, we weren't on great terms until yesterday."

"So Rainey had the balls to tell me and you didn't?"

"Pretty much." There's no anger, no humiliation, nothing in his tone but understanding.

And for some reason, the fact that he won't fight back pisses me the hell off even more. Combine that with the feeling of his hand on my arm and his threat to that man back in the club, and I'm full-on ready to come to blows. "We need to get one thing straight, Ridley, I do *not* belong to you. You hear me?"

He leans down, golden gaze darkening. "You're right. We do need to get something straight. You don't want to give what's between us a shot? Fine. That's your prerogative. I also understand that today was a mistake, but you should know—I'm a jealous fucking bastard, so if you're going to flaunt any relationships around me, just remember that it comes with consequences. You don't belong to me. I accept that. But, *an grá*, I do belong to you."

CHAPTER EIGHT

RACHEL

An grá. Love. I'd looked it up the second he left. Thank you, Google Translate. Love? Really? Love?

He doesn't even know me. And yet, I haven't been able to get his words out of my head. Even now, as I should be preparing for my shift, he's all I can think about.

"Freaking men," I growl as I finish filling my mug with coffee.

"Something on your mind?"

I glance up from coffee and meet the light brown eyes of my boss. "No, sorry, just annoyed. That's all."

He chuckles as he fills his mug. "I get that. Poor sucker probably doesn't realize just who he pissed off." Leaning back against the table, he faces me.

"Huh?"

"You said 'freaking men,'" he reminds me. "Therefore, I'm assuming it was one of my gender who pissed you off."

"Oh, yes." I laugh. "Sorry. A friend of mine was being an asshole."

"Not a boyfriend, then. Good to know."

His words catch me off guard, and I nearly choke on my coffee. I sputter, what was in my mouth either scorching my throat or coming out of my nose. In his defense, my boss doesn't laugh. He simply hands me a napkin and watches, eyes glittering with amusement as I attempt to regain control of my faculties.

"Sorry. I—"

"I caught you off guard, I understand. I never would have said anything except, well, I've always found you intriguing, and now that you know what I am—" He trails off, expression falling to something close to sadness. "Let's just say it's rather difficult for someone like me to find anything even mildly close to romance."

"I'm sorry. That must be hard."

He shrugs. "Just lonely. There are very few of my kind here in Billings, and as you can imagine, not being able to explain why I don't age is not a fun conversation." His defeated tone makes me incredibly sad for him.

Without thinking, I reach out and touch his arm. "I can't imagine."

He stares down at my hand then redirects his attention up at me before swallowing hard. "Thank you. All of this is just one massive pathetic way of pitying you into dinner."

I do belong to you. Ridley's words choose that exact moment to pop into my head, and it's all I can do to keep my magic from taking me to where it wants to go —wherever the hell he is. But I can't. And I won't.

"I'm not looking for a relationship."

"Not a relationship," he replies quickly. "Just friendship? A companionable dinner? Conversation with someone other than my house cat? And yes, I know that's weird. And, oh shit, I'm rambling." He sets his mug down and shakes his head. "It's just been a long time since I was able to have an honest conversation with someone."

I don't know whether it is because I'm so damned pissed off at Ridley or because I also could use a friendly dinner with no strings attached, but I nod. "That would be fine. As friends."

His expression completely morphs from mild sadness to complete joy. "Great, thanks. Tonight?"

"I get off at—"

"Eight. I know." His cheeks flush, and while it's

mildly creepy that he knew my schedule already, it is also kind of adorable.

"Eight it is," I say with a smile.

"Great. I can't wait." His phone buzzes in his pocket, so he withdraws it and, after checking the screen, mutters a curse. "Shit, I have to take this. See you tonight."

Then, he leaves me standing in the break room, knowing I likely just made a huge mistake.

THE REST of my shift went by smoothly, so by eight-fifteen, I'm standing outside of the hospital—and thanks to my new ability—I managed to go home, change, and be back within five minutes. Handy little bit of magic, to be sure.

"Is it safe to approach?"

His words wash over me, and it takes a hell of a lot of willpower to not lean back into him as he comes to a stop behind me. But then I remember his words and the way his eyes watch me, and I manage to remain standing straight.

I will *not* be owned. And whether he wants to admit it or not, Ridley believes his magic has some kind of claim to me. Soul-bound or not, my life does not belong to anyone but me. "What the hell are you doing here?"

"Coming to get you so we can practice your power."

"I don't need your help tonight."

"No?"

I turn to face him. "No. I have a date."

He steps back, eyes widening, nostrils flaring. "A date."

"Yes. With a man."

"Any particular person I know?"

"You ready?" Max chooses that exact moment to make his presence known.

Ridley turns. "Shifter."

Max's eyes widen. "How do you—"

"I'm a fae, you dumbass." He turns to me. "Really? You're going out with a shifter?"

"Yes." I stand my ground. He wants to keep secrets from me that have to do with my safety, then I'll keep shit from him. It's only fair, isn't it?

Ridley glares at me then turns to Max. "Hurt her and I'll fucking kill you." He disappears.

"I didn't realize you were so close with the fae."

"I don't want to talk about it. Do you still want to go?"

Max's shoulders relax. "Definitely. My car is over here."

I follow him over to a white sedan parked in the Chief of Medicine's spot, smiling kindly as he opens the passenger side door for me. After climbing inside, I take a few steadying deep breaths to try to calm my racing heart.

By the time Max is sliding in behind the wheel, I've

managed to put a perfectly calm exterior in place. "So, how long have you been in Billings?" I ask as he turns on the car.

"About twelve years," he replies. "I transferred from another hospital a few states away, tweaked my paperwork a little bit to appear younger, and, well, here we are." He guides the car out onto the street.

"How long do you stay in one place?"

"It depends on the threat level. For obvious reasons, I avoid areas with heavy hunter traffic, so when they start piling in, I take off."

"Not all hunters are bad though. I've met some good ones."

"Trust me, they're all bad. Varying levels, sure, but for a supernatural like me, they spell trouble."

"Rainey's all right."

"For now. But mark my words, the second she thinks I've stepped out of line—whether I have or not —she's coming for me."

I don't agree with him, though based on everything I know, I can understand why he would think that. After all, hunters are there to keep supernaturals in check. Their job is to literally put them down when they are harming humans.

"What about you?" he questions. "How did you get pulled into this world?"

"I saved a witch a few years back," I tell him honestly. "Since then, I've been helping supernaturals behind the scenes, aiding in whatever medical ailments their healing abilities cannot help."

He chuckles. "That's a big job."

"It is," I agree.

"What type of ailments? I'm curious what abilities cannot heal."

"Really, just silver-related ones. For example, I've removed silver arrow heads from vampires, shifters, and witches alike, and stitched up life-threatening wounds to help aid the healing process. I've stitched up a lot of bite wounds on witches in particular."

His laughter grows. "I could see that; witches can be a bitchy bunch."

"Not all of them," I tell him, my thoughts drifting to Bronywyn and Delaney.

"Not all of them," he agrees. "But I've crossed paths with more than a handful of witches who'd just as soon put me down than let me cross their path."

"Fair enough," I reply with an easy smile.

"Must have been a shock for you, though, to be pulled into this world at such a high capacity."

"It was, but I'm doing good, and that's all I care about."

"And the fae?"

What part of I don't want to talk about it don't you understand? "He's a bit more complicated."

Max's grin fades. "I can see that. Are you two in a relationship?"

"He thinks we are. Apparently, they can have only

one mate, and he thinks that's me," Should I be telling Max all of this? Probably not, but he's never been anything but kind to me ever since I came to work for the hospital and he was just a co-worker. "Anyway, as I told you, I'm not looking for a relationship."

He lets out a low whistle. "That is a complication. Shaking a light fae, that's not going to be easy."

The way he says it—the tone, the wording—it bothers me. I can't begin to explain it, but the warning bells in my brain are deafening. Especially, as something between us grows, the air charges, making my stomach churn.

What the hell is happening?

"Oh, hang on, I have something for you." As he's driving with one hand, he reaches into his pocket and withdraws a shiny object he cradles in his palm. Then, he reaches across and touches it to the bare skin of my hand.

The moment it touches me, pain singes my hand. It climbs up my arm, my shoulders, down my chest, back, and finally—legs. Every part of me is on fire as I arch into the seat, sweat already beading on my skin. Panic sends my mind spiraling, my stomach twisting, and I fumble for the door handle. It doesn't budge, though.

I think of Ridley.

Of Bronywyn.

Of Rainey.

Anyone who I could dematerialize to, but nothing happens.

"Don't bother trying to dematerialize," Max tells me, though—it's no longer Max.

Somehow, I manage to turn my head despite it feeling like lead. Where a handsome man once sat, there is now a black-haired woman. She turns toward me and grins widely.

"I cannot wait to play with you. We are going to have so much fun." She reaches forward and cranks up the radio. A heavy metal band comes on as tears prick the corners of my eyes, and I regret every damned decision that brought me here.

In the hands of a dark fae, I realize my biggest mistake.

CHAPTER NINE
RIDLEY

The image of that fucking cat's hands on Rachel drives me bloody mad. In an attempt to curb my anger, I head out with Rainey and Elijah, though right now, they look nothing like themselves, thanks to Fearghas's potent glamour ability.

Unfortunately for me, I'd been looking to blow off some steam, but it seems all supernaturals have taken a fucking night off.

"This is great news, isn't it?" Rainey asks, hopefully.

"Not for me," I retort.

Both hunters turn to me. "Well, your bloodlust aside, it may mean the supernaturals are learning to respect the new council."

Elijah's words are nothing but a bandage over a much bigger problem. I've been around long enough to know that with every council change, there's a lull, but as soon as they get comfortable, the supernaturals will begin pressing boundaries.

And that's when chaos will break out again.

But I don't say that, because even in my foul fucking mood, I don't have the heart to rain on Rainey's parade. "I'm sure that's what it is," I agree.

Rainey stops in her tracks and turns to me. "What the hell is up your asshole?"

"Rach—" Pain. Blinding, searing agony, spreads up my arms, snaking through the lines of my soul-bound tattoos and into my brain.

Something is wrong. Very, very fucking wrong.

"Ridley?"

"Something is wrong. Rachel—" I choke out as I fall forward. She's terrified. I can feel the gut-wrenching panic as though it were my own. "Fuck." I struggle to breathe, my lungs feeling like they're closing in on me, and I don't know if it's because of my fear or hers.

"Where is she?'

I shake my head, trying to form a breath. With her in mind, I attempt to dematerialize, but the ability--it's gone. "I can't go to her."

Rainey's eyes widen, and Elijah regards me with concern. "What do you mean you can't go to her?"

"I can't dematerialize—" I think of someone else—anyone else—and the ground shifts. Cole jumps up from his couch as I appear in their living room.

"What the hell, Ridley?"

"What is it?" Delaney asks as she pushes to her feet, hands cradling her swollen belly.

"Rachel is in trouble." I vanish, appearing back in front of Rainey.

"Did you find her?"

I shake my head. Panic claws at my throat. "I can't get to her. Why the fuck can't I get to her?"

GATHERED in the living room of Bronywyn's house is bringing back memories I'd really have rather left behind for good. Planning for war is never an easy thing to do, but I honestly feel like we've had more than our fair share of loss, haven't we?

"What happened tonight?" Delaney asks, "Can you fill us in?"

"Rachel went on a date," I spit the word out like the fucking toxic poison it is.

"Date? I thought you two were—" Cole trails off at my glare.

"She went out with the fucking shifter from her work."

"The feline?" Rainey questions. I nod in return, not trusting myself to say anything helpful in that area. "Dammit, I told her to be careful around him. Why does no one ever listen to me?"

"Explain to us what happened. Why do you think she's in trouble?"

"She's in pain, scared, what the hell else do you need to know?"

"You sure you're not just jealous?" Fearghas questions.

I shift my glare to him. "I'm not fucking pathetic."

"Let's not add to our problems by you getting your ass kicked," Rainey says to Fearghas before turning to me. "You can tell all of those things?"

I raise my sleeves to remind them all of my ties to Rachel. "Yes."

Bronywyn gasps, so I glance down. The inky lines are moving along my skin, slithering like they have a life of their own. I shiver as a wave of pain slams into me and nearly knocks me to my knees, an ice pick to my already aching heart. "If you're not going to help me, at least, get the fuck out of my way." I start for the door, but Tarnley blurs to stand in front of me.

"We are going to help you." He shifts his gaze past me. "Right?"

"Of course," Rainey replies instantly. "We just need to know what we're dealing with. You sensed feline shifter too, right?" she asks me.

"Yes," I snarl.

"Then we know what we're dealing with. Is it possible he knew she was fae?" Bronywyn asks.

"She said she didn't tell him," Rainey informs us. "When she came to see me this morning," she adds when we all glance her way.

"I didn't know she went to see you."

"Clearly, you don't know everything she does," she shoots back at me.

"Did you know about this date?"

"No. But had I known, I still wouldn't have warned you if that's what you're asking." I open my mouth to argue, but she throws up her hand. "Look, for the record, I vouched for you not being an arrogant asshole. Don't go proving me wrong."

Her words force me to swallow my own. "None of this matters, anyway. We need to find them."

Rainey withdraws her cell. "I'll have Walker look the good doctor up, see if we can figure out where he took her. You, Elijah, and I will go to his place, Tarnley, Bronywyn, and Fearghas can check out her apartment." She presses the phone up to her ear as I drive the palm of my hand as hard against my chest as possible.

My entire body is aflame, each part of me knowing with absolute certainty that Rachel is in trouble.

She's hurting.

Terrified.

And for the second time in my life, I'm completely fucking helpless.

"You okay?"

I shake my head at Fearghas's question, still fucking pissed he thought jealousy would push me to this point. Then again, I likely would have asked the same of him. "No."

"We'll find her. This is not the same."

My head whips in his direction so fast I'm momentarily dizzy. "You will *not* bring that up right now."

Fearghas drops his voice, though I don't know why since everyone but Bronywyn will be able to hear him anyway. "Fine. But you need to keep your head. She's a fae; he's a shifter. She already has him overpowered."

"He's dosed her with iron, I'm sure of it."

Green eyes widening, Fearghas takes a step back and crosses his arms. "You really think he'd go that far?"

"It's the only explanation for why I can't get a read on her and for the fucking pain." I groan as my chest tightens.

"Are you going to be able to dematerialize?" Rainey asks, and I nod. "Great, then let's get going. I have an address for you." She hands the slip of paper to me, though I don't need it. Since I'm experienced, I don't have to have been somewhere in order to materialize there. I just have to focus on the person, and their draw will take me where I need to go. Perks of being a practiced fae, I suppose.

I'm alive, which means so is she. I tell myself the same thing, over and over again, in an attempt to keep me sane as I fight to get the image of my sister, broken, bloody, dead out of my head.

Reliving the past won't help this scenario. Not when I still have time to save Rachel.

I just hope that time doesn't run out before we can get to her.

Chapter Ten

Rachel

"Wake up, wake up, little fae."

Something cracks across my cheek, and pain reverberates through my jaw. I open my eyes, a painful feat given the massive headache I'm sporting, but after a few moments of blinking rapidly, my vision clears enough that I get a crisp picture of the dark-haired woman standing before me.

"There you are." She grins, showing off blackening teeth. "I wondered if you'd come to."

"She awake?"

"She is," she replies to the man who I've yet to see.

I swallow hard, trying to ease some of the panic. Freaking the fuck out won't help me now even if it does seem to be the most logical option for me at this point. "Who are you?"

"Me? Why, dear, my name is T. My incredibly sexy companion here is S."

"S T? How original," I croak, my throat burning like I swallowed acid.

Her grin spreads. "She's feisty. I like her."

Heavy footsteps are like a hammer drill in my brain as the man comes into view before me. Black boots covered in chains meet black leather pants hung low on a thin waist. His bare chest is covered in lacerations, some open and oozing, others halfway closed. "She's pretty, too," he coos as he runs a knuckle over my chest.

I turn my head, trying to get away from his touch as fear claws at my insides.

"Not that pretty." T pouts, jutting her full bottom lip out.

"Not nearly as pretty as you are, baby," the man whispers as he stands and grabs her by the back of her hair. He yanks her toward him and takes her mouth as she grips his arms, causing her fingers to slip into some open sores on his exposed arm.

My stomach churns, bile rising in my throat.

"What did you do with the real Max?" I ask her.

"He's part of my party, too." She gestures to the left, and I turn, gasping when I see the bare-chested man hung from his arms in the corner. "Such a fun little play toy."

"Anything for you, baby," S tells her as he slings a pale arm over her shoulders. "Now, you said this one is extra special. Why is that? She seems like a normal fae to me."

"She's not normal," T tells him, her grin spreading. "Because she is mated to another fae."

Oh no. I fucking told her everything.

"Mated?" The man looks to her for confirmation then back to me.

"Soul bound," she tells him.

He kneels in front of me, a new interest in his eyes as he reaches forward and brushes the ink on my arm. The moment his skin makes contact with me, he groans, the sexual sound bothering me far more than whatever the hell she stabbed me with in the car. "Yes, I can feel him now. Delicious. So much power. Royalty, if I'm right."

Royalty? "He's going to come for me," I tell them.

The woman laughs. "Unlikely after how pissed he was. How fucking pathetic he'd been. You should have seen it, S." She snaps her fingers and transforms, body shimmering until Ridley is standing in place.

Just the sight of him hurts me, especially when she mimics his broken expression when I'd told him I was going on a date.

I'd done it to hurt him, and for what reason? Because he hadn't told me about the dark fae?

I've never felt so damn small in my life.

The man reaches behind him and pulls out a blade.

I try to push back, try to tip my chair over, to get anywhere away from him, but I'm helpless, the chains binding me firmly. The cool blade presses into the ink of my tattoo, and he slices me wide open.

I scream, blinding agony taking over.

I'm turned inside out, and the man in front of me moans, his head falling backward as golden power shimmers around him. "Yes, yes, yes, fuck yes," he calls out.

Then, it stops and I watch in horror as the wounds on his body heal completely. "You are a treasure, bitch." He grips my chin and presses his lips to mine in a rough kiss. The bile breaks free, and I vomit, everything I've eaten in the last few hours coming up as my stomach spasms.

He laughs. T laughs, and they both watch me as my lap and chest become covered in puke.

"You will be a fun one. You did good, baby," he says to T. Then slings an arm around her shoulders and guides her toward the door. "Let's go have some fun, shall we?" He glances back at me. "I'll be back for you."

The second door closes, I cry out, my head hanging low as the sobs break through, my shoulders shaking heavily with my anguish. Not only did I endanger myself but Ridley too. Is that why he cut my tattoo? What if he killed him? Is that possible? Can you even kill a fae?

"Rachel?"

My attention shifts to the voice in the corner. "Max?"

He coughs. "Why are you—what are you?"

"I don't know. Are you okay?"

"Never better," he replies. "Why do they have you?"

"How long have you been here?" Have I talked to him at all?

"I don't actually know. I remember talking to you in my office, but then—it gets fuzzy."

"That was yesterday."

"Fuck, it feels like longer. Why are you here?"

"I'm a fae."

His brows draw together in confusion. "You were human, though?"

"I was. Can you not sense like other supernaturals can?"

"I don't bother trying these days since I do my best to hide my true self," he replies, voice gravelly. "Fuck, my chest hurts."

"What did they do to you?"

"They're stealing my magic," he says. "Do you not know what they are?"

"Dark fae, right?"

He nods. "Do you know anything about their kind?"

"No. I wasn't born."

Max mutters something I can't quite make out then takes a ragged breath. "Think of dark fae like supernatural black holes. They are pure chaos with the ability to mimic your biggest fears, regrets—it's how they manage to so perfectly mimic those they take the form of."

"What do they want from us?"

"They are going to drain us of our power," he tells me. "To heal S. You noticed his injuries?"

"Yes."

"I overheard them talking, and apparently, he was hit with an iron bullet. She got it out, but the residue left behind was eating him alive."

"But fae can heal, right?"

"Light fae can. Dark fae cannot. They lack that magic."

"So they steal it," I choke out, feeling a tear slipping down my cheek.

"Don't panic. You can dematerialize, right? You can get us out of here."

"I can't. I tried. She touched me with something and —" My throat constricts, the panic making it hard to breathe. Is this how I'm going to die? Chained to a chair in the dark?

Ridley's face swims into view. Bathed in sunlight, I can see him standing on the cliff outside of Greece right beside me. I've never been someone who believed in instant love. While supernatural mate bonds have changed my opinion on it, I do know that what I feel for him is a bit more complicated than that.

I'm attracted to him, sure.

But there's more. His being calls to me, making it

impossible to think of anything else when he comes into focus. A relationship with him could be heart-breaking, I know that much. But sitting here, knowing I will likely never see him again, makes me wish I would have—at the very least—given it a shot.

Not because I think it would have led somewhere else but because knowing I won't ever explore the depth of those feelings is soul-shattering.

"She probably infected you with some kind of toxin. What does it feel like?"

"My body aches," I manage.

"It can't be iron because, if it was, he wouldn't have been able to pull magic out of you. Likely she used some kind of paralytic."

"I can still move." I demonstrate by flexing my fingers.

"Magical paralytic. There are some herbs out there that basically trap a supernatural in their current form. For shifters, they can't change; for witches, no magic; vampires, no enhanced speed."

"And for fae, they can't dematerialize?"

"I don't know enough about it to give a definitive answer, but yes, I would assume so."

"What am I going to do?"

"Can you use your wings?"

"Wings?" I glance over at him. "What wings?"

He stares back at me. "How new are you?"

"Very," I reply. "You know that war that got publicized?"

"Couldn't have missed it."

"I died. A fae brought me back."

Max arches an eyebrow. "Your mate?"

"He thinks so."

"Damn, Rachel, that's—why didn't you tell me? That day in my office, why didn't you tell me what you were?"

"I'm still processing," I tell him.

"Okay. Fae have wings."

"Like actual wings?"

"Yes. Try to use them."

I close my eyes and try to will wings to open, which makes me feel foolish, but given the current circumstances, I would have hopped on one foot and done the chicken dance if it would get us out of here. But I feel nothing. "I can't. I don't know how to open them."

Max stares at me a moment then forces a smile. He looks exhausted, broken, and what little energy he had seems to be depleting quickly. "We'll figure something out," he promises. "Just keep trying."

I close my eyes again, but this time as I try to focus on finding my wings, all I can think about is Ridley.

Please find me.

CHAPTER ELEVEN
RIDLEY

"This guy has not been here for a bit," Rainey announces as she comes out of the bedroom. "Bed is made, coffee still on the counter."

I glance into the *World's Best Boss* mug. "Looks old," I add, noting the dead fly and dark ring around the top. Anger flashes through me, and I swipe my hand, sending the damned mug into the wall. It shatters, and dark liquid rains down.

"What the hell, Ridley!" Rainey snaps.

"Where the fuck are they?"

"I don't know, but breaking dishes won't help."

Elijah emerges from the hall. "Neighbors haven't seen him since yesterday morning. They said they don't think he came back last night because, typically, he stops in to help the woman get her husband out of his wheelchair and into bed, and he never showed up."

"Guy seems to be a real fucking prince, doesn't he?" I growl.

Ridley.

Rachel's voice fills my head, and I pause, freezing in place, so afraid that if I take a break, it will sever whatever connection we've made.

Awareness spreads through my body as I inhale deeply, a putrid stench filling my lungs. It has nothing to do with the apartment around me, meaning it *has* to be what she's sensing.

Please find me.

I'm fucking coming. I promise. I will the words back to her, not sure if she'll ever get them or if I'm imagining everything I'm feeling right now. For all I know, it's not even real, but it's something to hold on to, and right now, that's exactly what I need.

A flash of something runs through my mind,

A man in chains, bloody and bruised.

Another man kneeling, blade in hand. Body covered in sores.

"Ridley?"

"Not now," I tell Rainey. A woman, dark hair, grinning from beside him. And then it fucking hits me. The images fade away. "Oh, fuck." Fear envelopes me. "I know who has her," I tell Rainey.

"I thought we'd already covered it's the doctor."

"No. He's a captor too. She's being held by a dark fae. Dark hair, dark eyes—"

She turns to Elijah, and he snarls. "I bet it is."

"The same one as the succubus den?" I ask, and she nods in confirmation.

"I knew that bitch was going to come back to bite us." She shakes her head angrily. "So how do we find her?"

"I don't know. They could be anywhere. Here or in the Veil."

Her.

It's the only word that passes through my mind the moment I materialize in the basement of the hospital, holding a dying Walker in my arms. Dark hair pulled away from her face, she's a fucking vision of perfection as she pushes a gurney toward us.

"What do we have here?"

I don't move, don't breathe as I stare at her while my magic goes completely rabid beneath my skin. It slithers, crawling, unfurling in its attempt to break free and envelop her.

"Ridley." Bronywyn's voice barely makes it into my mind. "She's human."

Fire. There, in her eyes. Fight. "Yes," she replies. "And if she doesn't get your friend upstairs, he's going to die."

Walker. I recall our reason for being here and set him down. One final look at her, though, and I am in desperate need of freedom. I disappear, leaving the human behind me.

Greece in the dead of night is spectacular, but I barely note the bright stars as I plop down on the rock overlooking the ocean.

What in the hell was that? Pressing the heel of my hand to my chest, I attempt to alleviate the ache blossoming behind my sternum. Never, in my entire life, have I ever felt a connection like that.

According to our history, it's rare. So rare, in fact, that I believed it to be nothing but a foolish myth, much akin to humans and their 'love at first sight.'

It makes no damned sense though. She's human.

Human.

Mortal.

So why the hell did my soul choose her? It doesn't *matter, I remind myself as I attempt to shove the feelings away. As long as I steer clear, I'll be fine. The last fucking thing I want is to be bonded to anyone—least of all a bloody human. Their lifespans are nothing but a breath compared to mine.*

An insignificant blink of time compared to eternity.

MY EYES FLUTTER open to the sound of my phone buzzing. I glance over at the clock on my nightstand and note that I've been lying here for only forty minutes. Forty fucking minutes after spending all night scouring the city for remnants of a dark fae.

Nothing.

My phone goes off again, so I begrudgingly answer it. "What?"

"We might have something," is all Rainey says before disconnecting the call. I lunge to my feet, still fully dressed, and dematerialize, appearing right beside her.

She jumps. "Fuck, Ridley."

"What did you find?"

Walker clears his throat in the corner. "She's still in Billings," the psychic says.

"You've seen her?"

He nods. "It was brief, but I know she's here."

"Where is she?"

"That is where it gets a bit foggy. I know she's here, somewhere in the city, and that she's in danger. That's about all I got though."

I want to slam my fist into something—anything. But even as pissed as I am his power didn't deem it necessary to give us a full picture, it's still more than we had before. After all, Billings is a fuck ton smaller than the world combined with the Veil.

"I'm sorry, man. I wish I could give you more."

"It's something," I tell him.

"We put an APB out on his car, so uniforms are on the lookout for it. And," Rainey adds, "I called Delaney, and she is putting some bounty hunters on it, too. As the head of the council, she's got some sway, and they were all too happy to take out a dark fae."

"This is so fucked," I snarl as I turn away from them. "If I'd just been a bit more patient—" I trail off, considering all the ways I could have been different. "If I'd told her about the dark fae, she wouldn't have been so pissed."

No one corrects me because they know I'm right. My eyes find the detectives, and she nods. She damn well fucking knows I should have been the one to tell her.

"Why didn't you?" Bronywyn asks.

"She was already dealing with so much, hitting her with a 'you might be hunted because of what I made you' seemed like a shitty thing to do at the time. Especially since we weren't on great terms. I figured Rainey telling her would be enough."

"I agree with that; it would have been a lot to process," Bronywyn says. "But it should have been you. Trust is not something Rachel hands out on a whim. You have to earn it."

"Yes, yes, I get it I fucked things right up, can we move on?"

"Well, for the record, other than being pissed, she handled the news pretty well." Rainey crosses her arms.

I turn away, helplessness slowly killing me. "We'd

already dealt with so much. A dark fae seemed the last of my concerns. Especially since she didn't seem overly threatening."

Rainey snorts. "She tried to get Bronywyn and me to kill each other."

"After she pretended to be my mom," the witch adds. "I'd say she was pretty fucking threatening." Bronywyn's cell goes off, so she answers it, stepping away.

"We all make mistakes," Elijah says from the corner. "We'll find her, and then you can grovel. Worked for me." He winks at Rainey, and she rolls her eyes.

"You men. I swear, if you would spend more time telling the truth and less time hiding shit, we'd all get along a lot better."

Bronywyn returns to the group, cell in hand. "That was my dad. He tried to do a tracking spell on Rachel but it came up short. He's going to ask around, see if there's been any weird activity anywhere."

It's all I can do to not start fucking destroying everything around me.

"Guess we're going for a drive," Rainey says.

"Not fast enough," I tell her. "I can take three, and we can pop around along the outskirts. If I were a dark fae, I would want to be as far away from the Astors as possible. No offense."

"Actually, that was quite the compliment," Rainey replies. "Let's do this, then."

"I'm coming with you guys." Bronywyn steps forward.

"Elijah and I will take a car around," Tarnley offers.

"I'll head back to the station and keep my ear to the ground," Walker adds.

"Great." I clasp a hand on Rainey and the other on Bronywyn. "Team break."

CHAPTER TWELVE
RACHEL

The heavy door slams open, and I jump, the loud *smack* pulling me from the light sleep I'd fallen into.

"Morning!" T greets with a wide smile as she saunters into the room with S behind her. Already, he looks better, his skin less pale than it had been, his wounds little more than red scars.

"How are my favorite little batteries today?" he asks with a wide grin.

"Fuck. You," Max chokes out.

"Muzzle your pet," S orders.

T giggles and rushes forward, reaching down to pull off her belt.

"Leave him be!" I yell as she wraps it around his mouth and tightens it. He fights back against her, but chained and exhausted, he's no match.

"Shhh, beautiful. You should be worried about yourself," S whispers as he kneels before me. "You know, I never understood the whole settling down thing. But you—" He trails off and whistles. "You are a sight to behold."

"Fuck off, you sick bastard."

He chuckles and reaches behind him to withdraw his blade again. The sight of it terrorizes me as I consider what he could be doing to Ridley through me. "You know, I've had light fae before, plenty of times really, but never a mated fae. The taste of you, of your mate, it's decadent. So much power shared between you two I don't think I'll ever get enough."

"He's going to kill you when he finds you. And that's only if I don't get to you first."

The dark fae's smile spreads. "A lot of talk for a fae weighted down by iron."

"You don't know him."

"From what T told me, neither do you. Trouble in paradise?"

I don't justify his words with a response as I continue to glare at him. Damn, I wish I had my gun.

"Not that it matters either way. One final taste and I

should be good to dematerialize, which means I can get the hell out of here, and we can go play in the Veil. All of us." He grins back at T.

"If all you need is my magic, just take it, and go."

"Oh, honey." He scrapes the blade along my arm. "You are a never-ending source of power. There is no damned way I'm leaving you here. Besides, eventually, you'll learn to appreciate what I can offer you." He trails the blade down my arm and over my upper thigh. "We're going to have so much fun, you and I."

Max begins to cough and sputter, body thrashing violently. Chains clink as he seizes.

"Max!" I yell as I attempt to break free from my prison of iron. "Let me help him!"

"T. See to your pet."

"I don't know what's wrong!" she exclaims, looking at the both of us for help. "Let her stand, S, please!"

S groans. "Fine." He reaches forward to release the chains binding me to the chair. "But if you try anything, I will gut him for all to see. Understand?"

I nod frantically, my pulse racing so fast it's making me dizzy. If Max dies, I'll be all alone. I know it's selfish to think that way, but I don't want to be alone. Having someone here to talk to might be exactly what I need to remain grounded.

S clicks something to the right of my elbow, and the chains relax. All but the shackles binding my wrists are removed. The dark fae's hand closes around my upper arm, and he yanks me to my feet. The iron shackles still on my wrists bite into my skin with each movement. Tears spring to my eyes, but I take a steadying deep breath.

First, I need to make sure Max is okay. Then, I can worry about myself.

"Fix him!' T demands, yanking me from S's grasp and thrusting me at Max. I hit his chest with a heavy thud.

"Get out," he whispers into my ear.

I whirl on them. "I need warm water and wash-cloths. And a shot of adrenaline if you can manage one."

T disappears, but S doesn't move.

"Where the hell am I going to go?" I demand, showing off my wrists. "If you don't want him to die, get me a shot of adrenaline!"

He narrows his obsidian eyes on me then snarls before disappearing.

I waste no time. Rushing over to the wall directly to Max's right, I hit the button to drop him.

"You need to run," he tells me.

"Not without you." I kneel and help him wrap an arm around my shoulders then rush for the corner, ducking behind to hide in the shadows as we make our escape. The door to the right is just out of my grasp, and as my hand closes around the handle, my heart hammers in my chest.

"Here—"

Dammit. T's voice fills the warehouse, and I shove us further into the shadows.

"Bitch!" she screams. A few seconds later, all falls silent again. I risk peeking around the corner, but no one is there. Gripping the handle, I shove it open. I'm momentarily blinded by the bright sun, but as I blink rapidly, my vision clears.

"You need to leave me," Max urges. "You can move faster."

"No. Stop suggesting it." His muscled weight is substantial on my shoulders, but I will not break.

I try to dematerialize, but nothing happens. Likely because of the iron around my wrists. Holding him, I move as quickly as I can, one foot in front of the other, between the buildings. Mountains in the distance ease my worry that we left Billings, and I know that if I can just get to someone—anyone—I can find Ridley.

Then he can—I trip, falling forward onto the pavement. Max groans.

"I hear you, little fae!" T calls out.

Panic ices my veins, and I frantically search for a place to hide. Just to the right, a small alcove catches my attention. Quickly, I urge Max inside then immediately stack some empty cardboard boxes from the nearby dumpster in front of him. "You need to get in here too," he says, holding his side due to what I imagine are more than a few broken ribs.

"No. They'll find us faster that way. You stay hidden. I'll get help. Please, don't move."

He stares at me as though he's going to argue but finally nods. "Don't let them catch you."

"I won't." After setting the last box in place, I gently place some garbage in front of it. Then, I take off down the opposite side. "Screw you, bitch!" I yell back as I tuck into a corner. I need to get them away from Max. As soon as that happens—

"You can't hide from us!" S yells. "We can sense your magic." Moments after he says that, they both appear a few yards away. "If she gets away—"

"She won't."

"She'd better not," he growls as he disappears again.

I run, a full sprint between the buildings. My lungs burn, my muscles screaming in pain. I have literally no idea where I'm going or if I'm even anywhere near an exit, but I can't give up. If I have to run until my feet fall off, I'll do it.

My foot catches on uneven asphalt, and I stumble forward. The side of my face slams into the concrete, and pain explodes at the points of contact. Warm blood trickles from the wounds as I scramble to my feet, trying like hell to keep moving.

"I can smell your blood," he calls out. "Delicious."

He's too close. I choke on a sob and duck back into the shadows.

I'm surrounded.

There's nowhere to go.

Nowhere to run.

The alley around me begins to spin, and I close my

eyes to shove the panic-induced vertigo at bay. My body heats, and sweat beads at my temples as I repeat over and over again, *please don't see me.*

If they find me, I'm dead. But what's worse is that Ridley will suffer. After everything he's done for me, he will ultimately be the one to pay the price for my stupidity.

Pain, torture, mental torment, I'll take all of it if it means saving him from what I know is coming. Except, I also know my death will lead to his own.

I try again to free my wrists from the iron shackles binding them together. Every movement sends fresh pain up through my forearm, and struggling proves to be useless. The shackles are tight, further cementing what I fear will soon happen.

All because I was desperate for my freedom. Freedom that I always had—until now.

"Little fae, come out, come out wherever you are!" the woman calls out, her throaty voice amused. "We have so much to discuss!"

"Our time together is nowhere near done!" the man calls out.

I know he's right. Defeated, I tuck my knees up and remain silent, knowing the one good thing is that if they're here, Max is safe.

For now.

So here I sit, hoping, praying, my silent please the only company I have as I remain hidden from view.

But for how long? How long can I keep playing this

sadistic game of cat and mouse? I shut my eyes tightly, tears burning in the corners as I recall every choice, every moment that led me here. The domino effect that was initiated with a single gunshot wound to the chest.

Then my life was simple, ordinary, leading me to ask the one burning question I feel horrible for even considering—why the hell couldn't he just let me stay dead?

"Boo!" S appears in front of me, and I scream. He reaches forward and grips my hair, ripping me out of the corner, and throws me to the pavement. A bone in my wrist crunches, the odd angle combined with my body weight snapping it.

I cry out again, my sobs frantic. "Just leave me alone! You have what you want!"

S throws his head back and laughs. "That's rich. You know what I want? The ability to go to Faerie, to see where my kind was made. I want to eat delicious food, fuck beautiful women, and so far, I've been reduced to nothing but trash."

He stomps across the pavement for me as T appears beside him. "Where is my pet!" she screams.

"Gone," I tell her with a twisted smile.

She charges for me, but S stops her. "No. Go find him. He couldn't have gotten far."

With a growl, T disappears again, and S stalks toward me.

I scramble back as the asphalt digs into my skin beneath the shredded jeans I'm wearing. Something hard hits my back, and S withdraws his blade then kneels. "What do you say you give me another hit?"

"No!" I fight back, kicking, screaming, and trying to get away. One hand on my throat, though, and I begin to lose the fight.

My lungs burn, my vision fading as he tightens his grip on me. I barely feel the blade as it bites into my arm. But I absolutely feel the violent assault on my magic as it is ripped from my body.

Wind whooshes overhead.

S is ripped from my body, his own slamming into the wall behind him just before a man with massive obsidian wings lands in front of me. His back faces me, and I struggle to stand, using S's momentary distraction to get to my feet.

With the wall at my back, I steady myself.

"You will die for what you have done, leech," Ridley snarls. Then, without further hesitation, he reaches down, lifts S, and snaps his neck as though he weighed no more than a feather in his glorious wings.

I stumble, and Ridley whirls. The second I see his bright eyes on me, a sob rips from my chest, and I fall forward. He catches me, sinking to the pavement with me.

"I'm so sorry, Ridley," I tell him as he cradles me.

"You have nothing to apologize for. I should have protected you." His tone is panicked, his words rushed. His hands close around the iron, but it burns him. "Fuck. We need to get you out of here."

"We have to get Max."

"What? Seriously? He fucking abducted you!"

I shake my head. "Not him. There's another dark fae, a woman—T—she pretended to be him. But the real Max is injured; we have to get him."

Ridley swallows hard, and a muscle in his sharp jaw twitches. "Fine. Show me where he is." He reaches into his pocket and withdraws a cell phone. After tapping a contact, he presses it to his ear. "I have her," he says into the receiver.

I close my eyes and listen to the steady beating of his heart.

"She's hurt, but once we get the iron free, she should be okay. The man, Max, he wasn't the one who abducted her. I'm going to find him then drop a ping so you can come get us." He ends the call and stands, bringing me with him and swinging me up into his arms.

"We'll get you help soon," he promises.

"I'm so sorry, Ridley," I repeat. "I shouldn't have been so—"

"Save your apologies for when you're not fucking bleeding."

Chapter Thirteen

Rachel

"You're really lucky," Bronywyn tells me as she removes her blue exam gloves and tosses them into the trash. "Had they not found you in time, well, you know."

I swallow hard. I do know how bad it could have been if Ridley hadn't come crashing down into that alley like an avenging angel. "How's Max?" I question, hoping a change of subject will keep my heart from feeling like it was smashed to bits by a tire iron.

"He'll survive." She moves across the room to the door and pulls it open, so I follow her out into the hall, feeling the aching in my body with each movement. "You're going to hurt for a few days," she warns me. "Between the iron injuries and the magic ripped from you by the dark fae, you'll be lucky to be on your feet within the next few days."

"Good thing you have an in with your boss."

We both glance to the right as Max makes his way toward us, already looking better, thanks to his shifter healing. "How are you doing?"

"Great, thanks to you and Ridley? I think that was his name."

"It was," Bronywyn replies with a pointed look at me.

Yeah, I get it. I was a bitch. Too bad it took nearly dying to see that. "Well, this is me formally requesting a week off," I tell him.

"You've got it. Thanks again, Rachel. For not leaving me."

"You're welcome." I smile his way, and he clears his throat.

"Think we can talk for a second?"

"I'll see you later." Bronywyn waves as she excuses herself.

Max reaches up behind his neck and rubs as though trying to soothe an ache. "Listen, I know it's not any of my business and that we did both nearly die less than three hours ago, but since you did agree to it before, I want to know. Are you interested in going out sometime?"

Ridley crashes into my mind, his fear, anger, pain as I confronted him in front of the hospital. "I'm sorry, I'm not looking for a relationship. Which is what I told her when she was pretending to be you, too."

He smiles. "I get that. Friends?"

"Friends." I offer my hand. "See you in a week."

"See you then."

Not wanting any more awkwardness, I close my eyes and picture my apartment. The world around me disappears, and before I know it, I'm standing in my living room. Or, at least, I think it is. Before I can truly figure it out, the room begins to spin, and I groan, my stomach churning.

"Shit."

I start to go down, falling straight to the floor, but a hand on my elbow stops me. Warmth spreads through my body, an awareness that something I need is nearby.

Then, he comes into view. Dressed all in black, he is so damned beautiful it hurts my heart. Our gazes lock, and the world falls away, leaving only the two of us and nothing else.

All of my resistance, my fears, they disappeared in that alleyway when all I could think about was the man in front of me.

But before I can say any of that, he releases my arm.

"Probably shouldn't do that until you're back at a hundred percent."

"Probably," I reply. "I—"

"Listen," he interrupts. "I get it, I'm an ass, but what you did—running off with someone Rainey told you to be careful around—it was really fucking stupid."

"Max is not a bad guy."

Ridley's eyes flash golden. "Of course not. I would *never* insult your boyfriend."

There's the arrogant bastard I can't stand. "He's not my boyfriend," I shoot back.

"Sure as fuck fooled me. So, is it that you don't want a relationship at all? Or just with me?"

"Right now, it's the latter!" I shoot back. "From the instant we met, you've been ordering me around, telling me what I can and can't do, and it's infuriating!"

"You think it's a picnic for me? Have you even bothered to ask yourself what being soul bound to you means for me?"

I grind my teeth together.

"I didn't think so," he growls back. "But let me give you a quick summary. It means that my magic, my life, my soul, it's all tied to you. There is no happy ending for me, Rachel, no love of my life, no white fucking picket fence and children." He presses a palm to his chest. "I will always ache for you, yearn for what we could be, until the day you die and take me with you." He straightens. "And yes, I have pursued you, but not because of some fucking soul curse. Since the day I saw you in that hospital, you have haunted every second of my life. You are beautiful, determined, brave, strong, and nurturing. But above all, you are the biggest pain in my fucking ass. I wish that I could go back to the moment I met you and erase my own damned memory because you've brought me *nothing* but anguish."

He disappears.

I collapse onto my couch, my chest hurting with every single breath. Try as I might, I cannot push that night out of my head—the one when we really met is burned into my brain like a fresh tattoo.

STILL AWAKE, I can hear the thundering footsteps and harsh whispers of the others as they race down the stairs. While I can't make out exactly what they're saying, I can't imagine they'd be running down the stairs for nothing. Which can only mean one thing: the council found us.

Heart hammering, I jump out of bed and grab my gun with steady hands despite the adrenaline pumping through my system.

Then, with a deep breath, I pull open the door. Here's hoping you're not being an idiot, Rachel, *I whisper to myself as I rush down the stairs, gun ready.*

The moment I'm down in the bottom and take in the near-dozen warriors facing off with my friends, I raise my firearm, prepared to defend them with every bullet in my gun.

But before I can fully process what's happening, the man in front of me disappears.

"And just what are you doing here, gorgeous?" A mascu-

line voice sends shivers up my spine as his hot breath washes over my bare shoulders. He isn't even touching me, but it is as though his words are a gentle caress I don't even want to begin to understand.

"Calm down, Ridley. You met her before." Rainey's voice is barely discernable over the hammering of my heart that has absolutely nothing to do with adrenaline now.

The man moves around, stopping just in front of me. As soon as I realize who he is, I lower my weapon.

"I know who she is," he tells Rainey, though his gaze never leaves mine. "What I am asking is why the hell she's here?"

His pissed-off glare snaps me out of the pathetic lust I felt just a second ago. I've dealt with plenty of assholes like him, dated more than my fair share. The last thing I'm going to do is let a man tell me where I should or shouldn't be.

"She's here because she wants to help," I snap back at him.

"She's being targeted by the council," Tarnley interjects.

The vampire's words get the attention of the man before me, and he spins away from me to face them, his rage potent in the air surrounding him. "What the bloody hell do you mean she's being targeted?"

"She helped us, saved Walker by going up against three vampires," Tarnley replies.

The man turns back to me. "Do you want to die?" he demands. "This is no place for a human."

No place for a human. Damn, I can't wait to prove him

wrong. I take a step closer, and the man growls, retreating a step. "This is exactly where this human is going to stay, and you can move the hell on if you're unhappy with it." Even though I know it will be a mistake, I reach up and jab a finger into his chest. It's hard beneath my fingertip, and the contact sends a jolt through my body. But I'll be damned if I let him see it. "If you have a problem with that, you can get the hell over yourself."

He glares down at me, cheeks red, his handsome face tight in anger. I wait for his argument, but it never comes. After a moment, he surprises me and takes a step back.

With a deep breath, I face Bronywyn. "I'm sorry for the gun. I wasn't sure if it was the council."

The man snorts. "And yet you came running down to protect us—ballsy—woman. Very ballsy. Or, perhaps, fool-ish?" He turns away, giving me a full view of his profile. With a sharp nose and strong jaw, he's the most attractive man I've ever seen.

Why the hell are the pretty ones such raging assholes?

"I'm assuming things have only gotten worse in my absence?" he asks the others, and I do my best to refocus on the current state of things.

"You'd be assuming correctly," Tarnley replies.

"The council sent vampires after the psychic?"

Rainey's fiancé—Elijah—nods. "The council sent four vampires after him. They killed a bunch of hospital staff and patients."

The man's face contorts in rage again, and he shakes his head in disbelief. "Fucking assholes."

"Rachel managed to kill three of them, pumped them full of silver." Rainey glances at me.

"It was nothing," I reply, heat rushing to my cheeks in embarrassment. I've never been one for the center of attention, and still, I'd rather sing and tap dance on stage than be standing here right now. Because the man before me? He's glaring at me as though he's a lion and I'm the thorn in his paw. I may not know much about this world, but I do know, without a doubt, he is not someone I ever want to focus on me.

Because he has the power to devastate my carefully crafted world in the blink of an eye.

CHAPTER FOURTEEN
RACHEL

Five days.

It's been five endless days since I last saw Ridley. He hasn't come by, and at first, I was trying to give him space. Space that only lasted about a day and a half before I tried to materialize to him. It proved pointless, though, because it didn't work.

Every time I arrived where my magic thought he was, there was no Ridley anywhere to be found. To be honest, even though I know it's irrational and he has every right to avoid me, it's pissing me off.

I'll own the fact that I forced distance, that I pushed him away, but he had a part to play too. The part of the egotistical asshole—my doorbell chimes, thankfully interrupting my thoughts.

Grumbling, I push up and wrap my hand around the door handle to pull it open. Bronywyn holds up a bag of what smells suspiciously like tacos, and smiles. "Thought you could use some company."

"From you or the tacos?" I joke.

"Both." She moves past me and into my apartment, heading straight for the couch. I follow, plopping down beside her.

"How are you feeling?"

"Normal." I lift my sleeve and show her my tattoos. "Mostly, anyway."

Her brows draw together, and she gently touches the huge scar severing the lines of one of my tattoos. "That's strange. What does Ridley say about it?"

"I wouldn't know."

She looks honestly surprised as she stops messing with the tacos and turns her full attention to me. "You haven't seen him?"

"No. I figured he was out of town or maybe in Faerie. You said time moves differently there, right?"

She continues to stare at me. "He's still in Billings," she tells me. "He's been going out on hunts with Rainey and Elijah almost nightly."

I ball my fists up, tightening them so much my

fingernails bite into the soft flesh of my palm. "Are you serious?"

"Yes. I'm sorry. I thought you knew."

Groaning, I sink back into my cushions. "I think I might have screwed up."

"Hold, please."

She reaches into the bag of tacos and hands me one. I take it, though I don't immediately unwrap it.

"Tell me what happened."

"You know what happened."

"I know that he was into you. You died. He rescued you. You freaked out, tried to date your boss to make him jealous, nearly died, and now we're here."

"Way to sum it up," I joke.

"I thought so," she replies around a mouthful of taco.

"We didn't know each other super well before you brought Walker to me," I start. "I've been in quite a few shitty relationships over the years, one arrogant prick after the next—you know how it goes, and then I ended up with the one I thought was going to be perfect. Handsome, smart, capable, all those things that should have made up the bones of a fairy tale." My thoughts darken as I recall the man I'd once believed would be my happily-ever-after. "Not too long into the relationship, he got really controlling. I didn't belong at the hospital. Working was for men. Wouldn't I be happy raising a family? No, I couldn't go out with friends because it was inappropriate and reflected poorly on him and our relationship."

"He sounds like a real prince," she replies dryly.

"Oh yeah, I know how to pick them." I fall silent, taking a beat to process, recalling the exact moment I woke up and realized I'd completely lost myself. "Long story short, I realized all too quickly that I'd let this asshole run nearly every aspect of my life. I'd quit going out with my friends, stopped reading because he didn't enjoy it, and if I read while he was with me, it was rude. I changed every single aspect of my personality for this beautiful man who never thought I was capable of anything more than bearing his children and putting food on the table." Taking a deep breath, I begin to fidget with the paper wrapper wrapped around the taco. "When I realized it, I still didn't leave. Instead, I confronted him about it, and he slapped me. Right across the face."

The glass on my table breaks, and I jump.

"Shit, sorry, magic got away from me."

With a laugh, I get off the couch and kneel with her. Together, we work on picking up the shards of what had once been a crystal bowl gifted to me by the family of a patient. As soon as it's done, we take our seats on the couch.

"Did you castrate the fucker?" Bronywyn demands.

I shake my head. "I packed my stuff and left. It could have been worse, I know that, and while I'm not emotionally scarred from it, I never, ever wanted to be with another man who tried to dictate my life."

"Which is exactly what Ridley did when you two first met."

"And this bond between us, I didn't ask for it."

"Ridley is a lot of things," Bronywyn starts. "But I don't get a controlling vibe from him. The fact is you were human, Rachel, and as it turns out, being a human in a supernatural world is not a great thing most of the time."

She's not wrong. Hell, I ended up dead. "I know that. Trust me, I do."

"What has he done since you came back? Has he been bossy?"

That's the part that makes me feel insane. He really *has been* better since I came back. But I'm so used to expecting him to be an ass that I can't move on. "You know how someone you hate can do something super ordinary and it will annoy you?"

"You hate Ridley?"

"No. Of course not, but he annoyed the shit out of me when we first met. I was already feeling vulnerable, given my lack of supernatural abilities, and he was making me feel worse. Constantly."

"He was trying to protect you," she defends.

"I know that, and given what happened to me, I understand why, but it still annoyed me."

"You didn't answer my question, though. Has he been acting the same since you came back?"

I sigh. "No. Not really. I mean, a little, I guess, but after what happened, I imagine that has a lot more to do with trying to protect me until I'm ready than trying to shield me from the world."

"Exactly. And something else—mated bonds are incredibly powerful. That power, it's not easy to control for most."

I think of that morning when I'd appeared in the club. "Tell me about it."

"If you want my advice—"

"Which I do," I interrupt.

She flashes a smile. "Good, because you're about to get it." She plucks a tomato from the top of her taco. "Anyway, you need to take what you just told me and talk to him. I think you'll be surprised by the response."

"I'm not damaged," I tell her. "I just don't get into relationships with arrogant men."

"Rachel, come on, all men are arrogant. Some just know how to handle themselves better than others. Your ex was a dickhead, but that doesn't mean all men are."

"I know they're not."

"And if you're anything like me, you'd be bored as crap with someone who didn't challenge you. Ridley? He's going to challenge you daily."

I snort and unwrap the taco. "He will. It's more than that, though. The idea that my entire life has now been laid out before me, I don't like it."

"I get that," she replies. "But leaving you dead wasn't an option. You should have seen him, Rachel."

"I know. I've heard." I sigh, still staring down at the now unwrapped taco I've yet to touch. "I wish I knew whether his feelings were real."

"Listen, out of everyone you know, I am more than qualified to have this particular conversation with you." She sets her taco aside and turns to face me. "When I bonded myself to Tarnley to save him, much in the way Ridley did with you, I literally had zero clue what to expect. While I am not fae, I can tell you that, from my experience, there has to be something already there for the bond to attach to. Does the fact that his feelings developed quickly make them any less real?"

I consider her words and try to see things from his point of view. For him, this is normal, right? Supernaturals mate all the time, so for him, this would be totally typical. But I grew up human, and according to everything I know, there is no spectacular show of fireworks, no massive 'I love you' after the first scene. At least, not when something is real.

"Also, you should know, for a fae, this connection the two of you share? It's really, really rare and caught him completely off guard. I can tell you that he was not happy with it, either."

"You think what he feels is real?"

"I think what he feels confuses the shit out of him." She reaches forward and touches my hand, so I look up at her. "Ridley is not a bad guy, Rachel. Had he been, he never would have stuck around and helped us."

"He dated an evil witch."

She chuckles. "True, but he didn't know what she was, and as soon as he did, he helped us put her down. Something not a lot of people would do. Sacrificing who you love for the greater good—it's not a great scenario for anyone."

"Love? He loved her?" I never met Lucy—that fight was over before I fully came into the picture—but I've heard enough about the damage she did to know she was a monster. A power-hungry, soulless monster.

"Again, before he knew what she was. Lucy was an integral part of our community. From the outside looking in, she was a good person. When affection gets in the way, it's easy to be tricked, right?"

My own situation—granted much, much less serious—comes to mind. I'd really believed Michael was a good man. He'd had good friends, a solid family, I never saw the manipulation coming, so to believe Ridley could have gone through something similar with Lucy, it honestly helps me see him in a different light.

"Like I said, you two are having very similar conversations with other people, and you need to be having them with each other."

"He's ignoring me now," I tell her, "dematerializing before I even get there."

She snorts. "He likely senses you coming. The air shifts a bit when a fae dematerializes."

"Really?"

"We discovered that when Fearghas started popping up everywhere."

"Then perhaps I should arrive in a different way."

"I think that's a solid plan." Her grin spreads. "Want a ride?"

CHAPTER FIFTEEN
RIDLEY

My legs are propped on my coffee table as I stare blankly at my screen. *Scrubs* has been on my binge list this week, and I'm nearly at the end of the second season. Other than this amazing way to pass the time, I'm still sore from a fight last night that resulted in me taking a bullet to the shoulder and then having to listen—repeatedly—to Fearghas announcing how he's apparently the only bulletproof fae in our little gang of misfits.

Bastard.

I have more than that to thank for my foul mood, though. My attempt at giving Rachel space has now turned into me being pissed off that I'm giving it to her and that either of us need it, anyway. Fate played a sick fucking joke on me by mating me to someone who hates me.

And for what reason?

I saved her—multiple times, risked my soul to bring her back from the dead, took her to Greece...so what the hell did I do to deserve her contempt?

Fucking nothing, that's what. I can understand her hesitance concerning me at first, but I wasn't saying anything that wasn't true.

She was human.

Humans die easily.

A fact she proved by dying, and yet, she is still pissed.

So here I sit, chest aching, ego bruised, body sore, watching re-runs of a show Fearghas claims is the greatest sitcom on television. While I disagree—I happen to be a *Friends* fan myself—I will admit it's pretty damn— Someone knocks on my door, interrupting my thoughts.

Thank fucking goodness because they're so damned monotonous even I'm bored.

Pushing up to my feet, I cross the apartment quickly and pull open the door where I'm greeted with the sight of Bronywyn, hand raised, purple magic snaking down her arms. But it's not her that pisses me off.

No, what enrages me is the woman standing behind her shield. "What the fuck are you doing?"

Bronywyn beams at me. "Just helping a friend out. See you later." She winks and heads down the hall, humming a happy little tune, completely unaware she just dropped a nuke on me.

Though, maybe she is aware and is sadistic enough to take enjoyment out of my pain.

"What happened to your shoulder?" Rachel questions, gesturing to the bandage visible because I don't have a shirt on. You know, because I wasn't fucking expecting company.

"I got shot. What do you want?"

Her gorgeous, soul-stealing eyes widen, and she takes a step forward. "Are you okay? When did you get shot?"

"What the hell do you want, Rachel? I'm busy."

She crosses her arms and disappears, appearing right behind me. Even without turning around, I can feel her, my own, personal weakness. Her heartbeat is a welcoming lullaby to my ears, but I shove it off. I already bared my damned soul for her, and she threw it back in my face.

"I want to talk to you."

After shutting the door with a heavy slam, I turn to face her and lean back against it. "If only there were little rectangle devices we could talk on."

"I tried calling you. Texting you. You never responded."

"Then that should have given you your answer."

Her cheeks flush, and my cock hardens. Fighting with her, it's an aphrodisiac, and I'm pretty sure that's twisted as fuck. "Would you stop being such an ass?"

"That's what I am, though, right? An asshole?"

"You're certainly acting like one."

"Why, Rachel, I do believe we have a pot-kettle situation here." Needing some space, I move past her and into the kitchen to grab a root beer from the fridge.

"Look. I didn't come here to fight." She moves into my kitchen, near enough to give me an up-close look at the golden flecks in her eyes. Flecks that appeared after I brought her back from the Veil. "I want to talk to you. Honestly."

"About what? How you despise me with no real reason to? Or how you continuously treat me like shit no matter what I do for you?"

The corner of her mouth twitches, and she closes her eyes tightly. "Look. I've dated arrogant men like you before. Men who act great on the surface and still managed to manipulate everything about my life until there was barely a shred of who I am left. I worked my ass off to get myself back, and I'm not willing to lose me. Not for anyone."

I know she means for her words to be some massive revelation like what happens in romantic comedies when the hero or heroine comes out with their backstory. There's always tears, a big forgiveness, and then happily ever after.

But fuck that.

"So you took your past baggage and piled it on me without even bothering to give me a chance to fuck up all on my own? Nice. Seems you have me all figured out, then. There's the door." I start to move past her, but she doesn't leave. Instead, she moves directly into my path.

"I did do that, and I'm sorry. What I did by going out with Max—it didn't start as a way to hurt you. But then you showed up and—"

"Fuck me, right?"

"It was wrong of me. I'd already told him—I mean her—that I didn't want a relationship. I'd agreed to a friendly dinner, that's all."

That particular admission does make me feel better, but I don't say anything. Truth be told, I'm prideful as fuck, and that blow took me to my knees.

"Turned out to be the dinner of a lifetime, too."

"I had literally no idea it wasn't really him."

"No, but you were pissed at me because of the dark fae threat I failed to mention, and then you go out and nearly get yourself killed. Let's push aside what it did to me mentally. Do you know what they did when they stole my power, Rachel? He drained me. Why do you think I had to drop in with my wings when I figured out where you were?"

Her eyes widen. "I thought I was talking to Max,

149

Ridley. I never would have told them about you otherwise."

I take a step back at the impact of her words slamming into me. "You told him what exactly?"

"That you thought I was your mate," she replies. "That's it. About you, I swear."

Standing this close to her, breathing her in, feeling the warmth of her body radiating toward me, it's all too fucking much to take. I can all but taste lips I've never felt, feel her body beneath my hands.

Even now, my fingers flex, reaching for what they will likely never touch.

Craving peace and hoping she won't follow me, I disappear, going to my favorite spot in the entire world.

And then she appears.

"Really? You're going to run?"

I groan. "Just happened to know where I was going?"

"I took a gamble. You said this was your favorite place, so here I am." She stalks toward me, bathed in the bright moonlight casting shadows over her face. She's fucking ethereal, so beautiful it lights up my entire world.

"Ruining it for me."

"I wasn't fair to you," she admits. "I recognize that, and I hate that it took nearly dying to see it. I'm sorry. I just, I didn't see how your feelings could be real, and the last thing I wanted was to be tossed aside when you realized that I wasn't who you wanted."

"I had no choice, either," I tell her. "I never wanted to be mated. A connection like this?" I gesture between us, hoping she'll understand the seriousness of our situation. "It's a weakness, and I'll be damned if I have any more of those."

"You loved Lucy."

I gape at her a moment, trying to figure out where Lucy fits into things. "Lucy was different."

"But you did love her."

"I thought I did," I admit. "But it wasn't an actual bond, and as it turns out, what I felt was only surface level anyway."

"But that doesn't make it any less real."

"No, it doesn't, but it made her a lot easier to get over. Well, that and the fact she tried to kill me and everyone I've come to actually give a shit about."

"Exactly, and our feelings aren't fictional just because a bond is what brought us together."

Her use of the phrase 'our feelings' does not go by me unnoticed, but I don't dare mention that or the fact that I wanted her before the bond—which she already knows. "It doesn't."

"No." She takes a step forward. "I'm not pretending to completely understand what's happening, but I do know that I want more of it."

I narrow my eyes at her. "I'm not an experiment."

"No, of course not, I just—"

Unable to help myself any longer, I cross the distance, grab the back of her head, and slam my mouth onto hers.

She starts to say something, but the words die on her tongue as she wraps her arms around my neck.

Fuck, she tastes like perfection. Her lips are soft beneath mine, and I slide my tongue over the seam and urge her to open them, to let me in. She does, and our tongues meet. She moans against my mouth, and my cock goes rock hard as all blood heads straight for fucking there.

I dematerialize us both, and without breaking the kiss, we appear in my room where I lay her back against the mattress. My body covers hers, resting right between legs I've wanted wrapped around my waist for *months.*

I press against her, and she arches up into me. So fucking perfectly molded to my body. I devour her mouth, my blood hammering within my veins as I fight to control myself in an attempt to not rip her clothes off and fuck her senseless.

I am a gentleman, after all.

Hand on my chest, she pushes me up. I stare down at her swollen lips, her glazed eyes. "I—I had not been expecting that," she stammers.

"Same."

"Can I sit up?"

"Shit. Yes. Sorry." I get off of her and help her sit up, taking a seat right beside her on the mattress. We sit in silence for a few minutes, and my mind wanders to all the ways she's probably never going to talk to me again.

"I want to see where this goes," she finally says. "But, as much as I hate myself for this, I want to take things slow."

It's a blow to my ego, that's for damned sure. "Slow."

"Yes. For you, this is normal, or somewhat, anyway. For me, it feels unrealistic because I've always believed that feelings were something that grew over time. I find a person I can spend time with, that I am attracted to, and then the feelings steadily increase."

"That's fair."

"But with us, shit, it went from zero to a hundred in four-point-four seconds." She takes a deep breath, so I take a shot and reach over to link my fingers with hers. Just the contact, the feel of her hand pressed against mine, it's paradise.

"Take it slow."

"Yes. I want to date."

Chuckling, I stare down at our hands, feeling lighter than I have ever since I saw her in that hospital basement. "I can do that."

She beams at me. "Good. Then, Ridley, I would like to go out. Dinner. Tomorrow."

CHAPTER SIXTEEN

RACHEL

"This is absolutely hopeless." I throw myself face-first onto my mattress like I'm a teenage girl about to go on her first date ever. It took finishing my hair and makeup to realize I have absolutely *nothing* first-date appropriate.

Unless, of course, that first date is beers and a pub where we play darts and high-five all night.

"It's not," Bronywyn calls back at me from my closet. "You just need something with a bit more pizazz."

"More like something—anything—other than

scrubs," Rainey adds from her spot in front of my dresser. She shuts the drawer and stands. "You literally have nothing but scrubs."

"As I said, hopeless," I groan.

"It is not," Delaney promises.

How my outfit choice got turned into a girls' afternoon I'll never understand, but I'm damn sure grateful. "Isn't it dumb to be going out when that other dark fae is still somewhere?"

"Aren't you the one who asked him out?" Delaney questions with a grin.

That's fair.

"We'll find your bestie," Rainey promises. "You just have a good time."

"That's if I ever make it out of here. He's supposed to be getting here in like—" I trail off and check the clock by my bed. "Thirty minutes, good to know."

"Relax, I called in backup on my way over here."

"That much faith in her, huh?" Delaney questions.

"I mean, come on, you've seen her closet," Rainey defends.

Before I can ask Bronywyn just who she called in, my door chimes go off, filling the room with happy, should-be welcoming sounds. "Is that him? Is he early? Why the hell am I nervous?"

Bronywyn's laugh follows her down the hall, and she calls out, "It's not him, calm down." The door opens near-soundlessly. "Thank you for coming."

"Anytime."

The familiar voice reaches me even in my bedroom. *Thank freaking goodness.* Eira steps into my room, looking fabulous as always even in her jeans, knee-high boots, and soft blue sweatshirt. "I come bearing gifts," she says with a grin as she holds up a white garment bag. "You are a bit taller than me, so I grabbed something longer."

Bronywyn carries over the bag and sets it down to unzip the fabric, revealing a stunning black dress. "This is going to look fantastic on you," Bronywyn says as she pulls it out and holds it up against me.

"This is stunning."

"It is. Now, go put it on so we can see." Rainey all but shoves me to the bathroom, so I do as I'm told and strip out of my robe. The silk is soft against my skin as I step into the dress. As I slide it up my body, I can't help but smile.

As soon as I've slipped the thin straps over my shoulders, I turn and study myself in the mirror.

"Well?" Rainey calls through the door. "Let's see it!"

With a deep breath, I smile at myself one last time then head out into the room. All four women grin at me, and Rainey offers a whistle.

"Looks good?" I ask.

Rainey nods. "I feel like we need to have *the talk*," she jokes.

"We're taking it slow."

"Yeah, okay, not in that dress you're not," she adds

with another wink. "You are an absolute knockout, Rachel."

Heat rushes to my cheeks.

"Leave your hair that way," Eira suggests. "The half-up look really suits that dress."

"Your tattoos look awesome, too." Delaney gestures to the inked lines trailing up both of my arms.

"Thanks, guys, I seriously cannot thank you enough."

"Shoes?" Delaney questions.

"Those, I have." Nearly giddy with joy, I make my way back into my closet before kneeling down and retrieving a pair of black pumps I've had hidden in the back since I bought them two years ago. I slip them on, so damned glad I didn't get rid of them when I went through my 'does it bring me joy' phase last year.

Hell yes, these bring me joy.

And tonight, seeing the look on Ridley's face is going to make storing them this long totally worth it.

"Damn." Rainey nods appreciatively.

"Agreed," Bronywyn adds.

Both Delaney and Eira simply nod in agreement.

"Thank you for the dress," I tell Eira. "So much. I promise to take good care of it."

"Honey, that dress is all yours."

"No, you can't give this to me—"

"I can," she interrupts. "There is no way I would ever feel good in it after seeing how fantastic you look." She winks, and I want to cry. My throat tightens, and my chest grows heavy with joy. How I went the last half-decade with literally no friends I'll never know.

Girlfriends are the best.

Someone rings the doorbell again, sending my heart into a nervous somersault.

"He's here!" Rainey exclaims.

"You've got this!" Bronywyn offers.

"Have fun!" Delaney calls out.

"Knock him dead," Eira adds with a wink.

My jelly legs somehow manage to carry me to the door where my sweat-slick palm closes around the handle and somehow manages to open it. Which is the precise moment I am struck stupid.

On the other side, Ridley is dressed in a black suit with a black shirt and a black satin tie. His hair is perfectly styled, his face clean-shaven. To summarize? I'm not entirely sure how I'm supposed to stick with my 'take it slow' mentality when I want to rip his clothes off and have him bend me over my kitchen island.

Which, thanks to my overactive imagination, has now given me way too many ideas.

"You look, fuck, Rachel."

"That's a shit compliment," Rainey announces as she comes behind me.

Ridley looks stunned, and the sight of it has me stifling a laugh.

"Rainey, I didn't know you were here."

"Clearly, or you would have managed something a

bit more romantic than the word 'fuck.'" She steps around me and heads out into the hall, which makes way for Delaney, Bronywyn, and Eira to follow.

They don't say anything, but when they get past him, there are lots of silent *ooohs* and *ahhhs* coming my way before they all disappear down the hall.

"Party tonight?"

"Something like that. Do you want to come in?"

His gaze drinks me in, sending my pulse skyrocketing to a level that can't be safe. "To be completely honest? I would love to, but if I go in there, I don't know that we'll make it back out, and I really, really want to show you off tonight."

"You know, I do have self-restraint."

He leans in and presses his lips to my cheek then hovers just above my skin. "But I don't, and I can be very, very persuasive."

I swallow hard at the heat pooling in my belly as lust slams into my body. "Fair enough. Let's go out." I close the door quickly before I have time to change my mind. Then I face him again. He's watching me, eyebrow raised, looking way too damned hot for anyone's own good.

"Ready?"

"Yes." I start down the hall and then stop. "Wait, no." Turning on my heel, I march back into my apartment to retrieve my purse, phone, and keys. Then, I move back out into the hall and try like hell not to make eye contact because, for some reason, I've lost every bit of confidence I've spent a lifetime obtaining. "Now I'm ready."

He chuckles, the deep sound washing over me. What the hell is it about his voice that makes me want to drool? "I have quite the evening planned for you, but first, I need to know, does this building have cameras?"

"Not in the halls. Wh—" My words are cut off when he takes my mouth in a knee-shaking, muscle-melting, swoon-worthy kiss that has me melting into a puddle of satin. My back meets the wall, and I wrap both arms around his neck, pinning him to me so even if he wanted to pull away, he'd have to struggle.

I want all of him.

Every single arrogant bit of him, and it's driving me absolutely wild.

After a kiss that didn't last nearly long enough, he pulls away and rests his forehead against mine as we both struggle to catch our breath. "I've been wanting to do that since I saw you in that doorway."

"I'm really glad you did."

With a grin, he drops his head and kisses me one more time, a quick peck that's just enough to make my knees shake. "Time to go."

The world falls away for a moment as my stomach drops, much like it does when you're on a heavy drop at a carnival. Within a heartbeat, though, we're rematerializing in the center of a dimly lit room.

"Look up," Ridley whispers.

I do as he says and gasp. Above our heads, the glass

ceiling is a window into a crystal blue ocean. Rays of the sun just beginning to shine through make it easy to see the fish happily swimming above—and around us.

"An underwater hotel off Rangali Island."

"I honestly don't know what to say."

"Here, sit." He guides me to a panoramic room adorned with two seats, a table, and a silver tray covered with a matching dome.

I slide into my chair, still awe-struck by the gorgeous view less than two feet from my face. "This is amazing."

"It's pretty neat. The pictures really didn't do it justice." He shrugs out of his jacket then sits down beside me. "I hope it's okay, but given the time difference, we are having breakfast rather than dinner." He lifts the dome, and my stomach rumbles, reminding me I've had nothing but a protein shake all day.

And as I eye the gorgeous arrangement of scones and fresh fruit, my mouth waters. "This is perfect, Ridley."

"You didn't strike me as the go out to dinner and a movie type."

"Well," I start before plucking a plump grape from the tray. "While I do love a good movie, you would be right about the dinner part. I'm not a fan of forced conversation, and when you are sitting across from someone, it becomes a necessity so you can avoid staring awkwardly into their eyes."

He throws his head back and laughs then reaches

over and grabs a scone. "I completely agree. Though, I will admit, I haven't been on many dates."

"No?"

He shakes his head. "Typically, it's always been a 'pass the time arrangement,' though there was one woman—a fae from my home—that I was rather serious with when I'd been younger."

"What happened?"

"I realized Faerie was not where I wanted to spend my life, and she couldn't bear the thought of leaving. Truth be told, we're better off friends anyway. No one else can look after my brother like she does."

"Rafferty? I think that's what his name is, right?"

Ridley snorts. "That would be correct, though it's not just Raffe. Honestly, he's the only sibling I have left I give a shit about." His mood darkens, a heavy shift in the air that I feel all the way down to my bones.

Even as I know I should proceed with caution, I can't help myself. "You have other siblings?"

He nods. "Another brother; he's a piece of shit though. Taranus is nothing but a stain on our family. Why Rafferty bothers putting up with him I'll never know." Ridley falls silent, his gaze shifting from the ocean beyond the glass to the fruit. "And I, uh, I had a sister. "

Had. My heart aches for him as a wave of pain shoots through my chest. "What happened?"

"She was killed. Back in Faerie."

"Oh, Ridley."

"It was a long time ago, but that's why I left. I needed space from my family. They were just trying to move on, and I wasn't ready. I'll never be ready."

Unsure what else to do, I reach over and rest my hand over his. He stares down at it then smiles tightly. "It was a long time ago."

"Time doesn't help everything."

"True." He turns away from me, but I don't move my hand. Instead, we sit together, fingers interlocked, as we stare out at the ocean that grows brighter and brighter by the second.

CHAPTER SEVENTEEN
RIDLEY

"I'm an only child," Rachel tells me with a sigh as she drinks a mug of steaming coffee room service delivered a few minutes ago.

"How was that?"

"Lonely," she admits. "But to be honest, probably better for everyone since my parents worked pretty much constantly."

"Were they doctors too?" I'm desperate to know everything about her, which is the reason I brought her here instead of a traditional restaurant. There, we would be surrounded by other people and forced to follow the normal timeline for closing.

But here, it's already a brand-new day, and we're completely secluded, giving us the chance to talk about anything and everything all at once.

"No, my dad was a software developer, and my mom had her own veterinarian office."

I don't miss that she used past tense, but I don't mention it. As someone who has dealt with loss, I always err on the side of caution when talking to someone else, mainly because I don't like to discuss it. "Forged your own path, huh?" I take a drink of my coffee, savoring the potent flavors of the locally roasted coffee beans.

She kicks off her heels and tucks her legs up into the chair, looking completely relaxed and keeping me completely enthralled. So fucking beautiful. "I did. They always pushed me to be whatever I wanted to be, whether it was the ballerina, the firefighter, or the superhero." She chuckles softly and smiles wistfully. "They died a few years back," she tells me sadly. "They'd been on their dream vacation, sailing a boat around the world to celebrate their retirement, and some weather came out of nowhere. They went down with the boat."

My chest aches for her and the grief I can feel through our bond. Pain is something I understand all too well, and I would never wish it on anyone. "I'm sorry."

She shrugs. "They died doing what they loved, and while I try not to focus on the details of it, I'm glad I got the two best parents while I did."

A school of fish move in front of the thick glass, swimming quickly, some smaller ones darting around them. It's far more magical than I could have imagined, sitting here with her beneath the ocean.

"I took a boat out last summer," she tells me. "In celebration of them. Stayed out for a few days in sight of the coast, but it really was a lot of fun." When she glances my way, I see the shimmer of tears in her eyes. "I didn't want to spend my life afraid of the water, so I forced myself to go out."

"You are seriously the bravest person I've ever met."

She snorts. "I don't know about that."

"You were a human woman faced with an impossible decision, and instead of hiding, you stood as a shield in front of a man you barely knew against four vampires. And let's not forget you charging down the stairs, gun hot, ready to take me out."

Her cheeks flush with crimson. "Don't remind me. That was embarrassing."

"Embarrassing? I'd say enthralling. You captivated me that day."

The color in her cheeks darkens when she turns to me. "You sure had a funny way of showing it."

"I was so caught off guard; all I could think about was taking you somewhere the ugliness of the war wouldn't touch you."

"I'm not built that way," she tells me.

"I know that—now. Admittedly I was a bit of an ass."

"A bit?" Eyebrow arched, she studies me.

"Fine. Maybe more than a bit. But you took me by surprise. I've been alive for so long I can't even remember, and you are the first person I've ever had that reaction to."

"What did it feel like?"

I fall silent as I try to put into words the earth-shaking, world-altering, bone-deep reaction I had to her. "Like my body was on fire and you were the only person who could make the pain stop." Her mouth falls open, and I swallow hard. "As though, if I didn't get close to you I would cease to exist. At least, that's the closest I can get to describing it." Feeling incredibly awkward, I get to my feet. "More coffee?"

She stands too, and when she reaches out and wraps slender fingers around my forearm, I close my eyes, savoring the feel of her hand on me. I should be embarrassed. Shit, it's pathetic the control she has over me.

I never understood Fearghas's need to be near Eira all the time, but now? I completely fucking get it. When you find the other half of your soul, the other part of you, being without is just not an option.

No matter what.

Her scent invades my senses as she steps closer, and I stand completely still, savoring every heartbeat of this moment. Soft lips press against mine, and it's all I can do to not completely lose it. Sensing her desire for control, I let her take the lead, though I wrap an arm around her waist and pull her in closer, the need to touch too damned strong to deny.

The tenderness of the kiss, it undoes me in ways I never thought would be possible, and when she pulls away, I'm left wanting more—so much more.

"I'm sorry I never gave you a chance."

I open my eyes. "To be fair, I likely wouldn't have given me one, either."

Her smile lights up my world. "This has been amazing."

"I wanted to spend more than an hour with you," I admit. "And I really wanted to be alone."

She arches an eyebrow. "You hoping to get lucky?"

"I mean, I wouldn't say no." I wink, not wanting to admit that for the first time in my life, that had not actually been on my mind. Damn woman is changing me, and I fucking love it. "But we're taking things slow." I take her hand and pull her through our underwater haven, stopping right before the closed closet in the master bedroom.

"What am I going to find in there?" she asks warily.

"An entire day of adventure that has nothing to do with life-or-death situations."

Not needing anything else, she pulls it open, revealing the bathing suits in various styles I paid the assistant manager to pick out. "I did not pick these out, and to be honest, I have no idea what is in there. But the woman who shopped for them assured me she'd get different styles."

Rachel beams up at me. "This is great. What are we doing?"

"We're going to spend the day being normal," I tell her. "And with that said, I am going to leave this room and go get changed myself. See you in a few." I wink at her and close the doors behind me. Then, like a lovesick teenager, I take a deep breath before heading to change myself.

"Okay, I'm coming out!" Rachel calls through the door fifteen minutes after I sat on the couch to wait for her. Trying *not* to think about a naked woman in the room next to me? Really damned difficult.

"I'm dressed!" I call back, shutting the book I'd been reading. I get to my feet as the doors open and she steps out.

"Damn." The breath is slammed from my lungs, my stomach somersaulting. Shit, my legs go weak as I take her in. Black and white striped triangles cover her breasts while matching bottoms sit low on her trim waist. Her creamy skin is on full display, her body so fucking perfect I want to fall to my knees and worship the ground she walks on.

"She had quite a few different styles, so if this won't

work for what we're doing, I can go change." She starts to turn, and I dematerialize, appearing in the doorway.

"No. Absolutely not."

Her cheeks turn pink. "You like it?"

"I honestly don't know how I'm going to keep my hands off of you," I tell her. "I may have to break the noses of some men today."

She laughs. "No one will have anything on you," she says, her gaze dropping to my bare chest then back up to my eyes.

Her approval brings a smile to my face. "Good to know. That may save their lives." Before I can do anything else, I take her hand and pull her toward the exit. Walking behind her might actually kill me at this point, so I stay in front, only glancing back when we're heading into the private elevator that will take us to the surface.

"Ready for adventure?"

She grins at me. "I'm up for anything."

And I know she truly is. "Then, let the adventure begin."

Chapter Eighteen

Rachel

After spending the entire day exploring all the beauty of this place, I'm beyond exhausted. Every second was worth it, though. The sun is steadily disappearing in the distance as I sit on the edge of the infinity pool situated above the underwater room.

To say I'm mesmerized by this place would be an understatement, but I never want to leave. If we could stay here, tucked away from the world forever, I'd be perfectly okay.

"Water?"

I glance back at Ridley, who thankfully has yet to put on a shirt, as he offers me a chilled bottle. "Thanks."

He sits down beside me, and I spare him a glance as he downs his water. Inked, taut skin that's sun-kissed from being out all day, all but steals my breath. He's so damn magnificent. Ethereally beautiful, and I honestly cannot get enough.

"What do you want to do tonight?"

"We have the place for tonight, too?"

He nods. "I figured we could do dinner then watch a movie? I'll sleep in the guest bedroom." The last part is added quickly as if he's worried I'm going to bolt.

"We can sleep in the same room," I tell him. "Doesn't mean we have to have sex."

He visibly relaxes. "Well, I, for one, am enjoying this whole take-it-slow thing. It's been fun."

I arch an eyebrow and turn to face him, propping one leg up on the edge of the infinity pool and leaving the other in the ocean. "You're enjoying not having sex?"

His wicked grin melts me. "I'm enjoying getting to know you, Rachel, because it's going to make the sex that much better."

Heat pools between my legs despite the cool water. He completely disarms me with a look. A single moment pinned beneath his gaze leaves me nothing but putty.

Swallowing hard, I'm unable to tear my gaze from

his as he leans in and presses his lips to the corner of my mouth, so close, and so damned far from where I want them. "Let's go order some room service." When he pulls away, I'm left wanting, yearning for his return.

Why the hell did I insist on taking it slow?

He swings his legs back into the pool and hops down, and the crystal water comes up to his bare chest. I follow suit, but before I can step down, he moves in close, coming to stand right between my legs.

My breath catches as I stare down into his bright gaze.

"You captivate me," he whispers.

Dammit. I lean down and press my lips to his in a tender kiss, my way of thanking him for the most amazing day, but that tenderness is lost as it quickly turns into something much, much more. My body aches, my need growing to a level that will surely kill me if I don't sate the burning desire in the pit of my stomach.

My hands find his hair as his arms wrap around my waist, pinning me against his hard body. Water envelops me as he pulls me off the ledge and into the pool with him. Cool tile meets my back, but I'm so damned hot I barely notice the chill.

His hard length presses against me, and I moan, but the sound is swallowed by his kiss. I'd pushed him to take it slow, to get to know me first, but now? All I can think about is shredding the thin fabric of our swim-suits and taking exactly what I want right now: him.

I slip my hands down from his hair and grip his muscled shoulders, letting my fingertips dig into his flesh.

Dammit.

Dammit.

Dammit.

I should pull away. Should put a stop to this now. But all rational thought disappears when he grinds against me again, and all that matters is my body pressed against his.

He pulls back and sucks in a shaky breath. "Fuck, we need to stop."

"Do we?" I question, He meets my gaze, his eyes heavy.

"We do. You wanted to take things slow; we are going to take things slow."

"I could be persuaded."

His chuckle vibrates through my body. "I've no doubt of that at the moment, but since that was not my intention of bringing you here, despite it being a hotel, I'm going to begrudgingly decline."

And if there was ever a time I wanted him more, it was now when, deep-rooted in our desire, he denies me because of something I wanted.

"Besides." He reaches up and tucks wet hair behind my ear. "We have eternity."

SLOWLY, I come awake. The warmth at my back brings a smile to my face, especially when I realize the TV is still on, the screen frozen on the landing page for the rom-com we fell asleep watching last night.

Popcorn has been discarded onto the nightstand beside me.

Last night was *everything* to me. Ridley and I laughed, talked, vented, and spent an entire evening getting to know each other in a way that goes a hell of a lot deeper than any of my previous relationships.

Even the four years that nearly led to marriage. With him, I don't worry about being guarded, about hiding pieces of me, because he accepts them all. Hell, the guy risked his soul to bring me back from the dead. I very much doubt he's going to care if I have a weird attachment to mismatched socks and orange Tic Tacs.

He groans and tightens his arm around me, pulling me in closer. When his lips go to my neck, a shiver runs up my spine though my body is anything but cold.

"Morning," he whispers before pressing a kiss to my shoulder blade.

I clear my throat. "Morning."

"You sleep okay?"

"More than."

Ridley's agreement is grunted as he kisses the base of my neck. The stubble on his chin from a day of not shaving scrapes deliciously. My nipples harden, and my body turns to little more than putty.

The last day has been amazing.

Perfect.

And I find that I'm no longer in need of the time I was so desperate for. I swallow hard and roll over onto my back. Ridley doesn't move, his arm still resting across my waist as he hovers above me, propped on an elbow.

Nerves wrecked, I reach up and cup the back of his neck. His nostrils flare, his pupils dilating, though he doesn't make a move toward me until I gently tug.

But when I do—his lips touch mine, the feverish need instantaneous. His hand tightens on my waist as my arms wrap around his neck. I need him—desperately. He moves, positioning himself between my legs, his hands splaying out on either side of my head.

With my stomach full of butterflies, I let my hands trail down his sides and to the bottom of his t-shirt. I grip the soft fabric between my fingers and gently, slowly pull it up, enjoying every bit of hot skin that is revealed.

His tongue is smooth against mine, his body hard.

When he releases my mouth so I can tug the shirt over his head, he hovers above me, staring down into my eyes. "Are you sure?" he questions, the muscles of his arms quivering. His entire body is rigid, his muscles poised as if he's doing everything he can to hold back.

"More than."

There are no follow-up questions, no moment to process. He takes my mouth again, this time with a desperation I mirror. My hands are all over his back, kneading the muscles, scraping against the skin. When I wrap my legs around his waist, I arch up, feeling his hard length pressing against me, and it is my complete undoing.

I need him.

Crave him.

And now, I will have him.

He pulls back and reaches down to remove the t-shirt I'm wearing. I sit up so he can pull it over my head. Then he tosses it to the side and remains kneeling between my legs as I lie back down. His eyes stare at me, traveling up and down my body.

"Fuck, you are a queen."

"You make me feel that way."

He leans down and whispers, "For eternity, *an grá*." He kisses me again then pulls away and drops his head to my neck, my shoulder, my breast. As though he's been perfectly trained to play my body like an expert, he pulls my nipple into his mouth, his teeth and tongue driving me damned wild.

I arch up as pleasure shoots through my body, sending every single nerve into overdrive until I'm sure I'm going to explode.

And he hasn't even touched the most tender part of me yet.

Leaving my breast, he trails his lips down my body, my stomach, my waist. He grips the sides of my shorts and slowly drags them down my body, taking his time to explore every inch of exposed skin. Never in my life have I ever felt so cherished. So wanted.

He climbs off the bed, and I lock gazes with him as he stands before my naked body. I'm completely vulnerable, and yet I feel more powerful.

"Your turn," I tell him.

He flashes a wicked grin. "I'm enjoying my view right now." But his hands go to the waistband of his shorts, and he shoves them down.

My mouth goes dry.

My pulse pounds.

He's *massive*. The butterflies in my stomach go rogue as he climbs back onto the bed and settles himself between my legs. His breath is hot on the inside of my thigh, and I have to fight every urge to arch up against his mouth, but I wait, letting him torment me with the sweetest kind of torture.

His tongue undoes me. He runs it over my clit, slowly at first, then closes his lips around me. Fireworks go off in my brain. The entire ocean could come crashing down on us, and I doubt either one of us would notice.

"Ridley— shit." I do arch up into him now, though the action is completely mindless, my body knowing it needs more. "Oh my— fuck, don't stop." I reach down and grip his hair, burying my fingers in the thick strands as he fucks me with his mouth.

My body comes to life beneath him, the orgasm ripping through me like a damned tsunami. Crying out,

I arch up, and he moves so damned fast I barely see him leave his spot between my legs before he's driving into me.

Ridley fills me completely, my body stretching around his hard length.

"Oh, my—you're so wet," he whispers as he pulls out then moves back in, drawing out my orgasm even as I'm already right back in the pleasure. I grip his shoulders as he moves inside of me, pulling out, thrusting in, the tempo a perfect match for the beat of my heart.

I never believed in true love. In soulmates.

But Ridley was made for me, and I'm never letting him go.

CHAPTER NINETEEN

RIDLEY

Coffee in hand, I prop myself up against the hood of Rachel's car like a teenager with a hard-on for his girlfriend. Shit, I might as well be since I seem to have a perpetual one anytime she's around. No matter how many times we've been together, how many nights we've shared over the last two weeks since that first morning, it's never enough.

She's magnificent, my mate.

I can feel her before she even steps out of the hospital, the awareness that the other half of me is near enough to send my heart into overdrive.

When she steps out, my world brightens. Her gaze travels over the parking lot, landing on me, and she smiles. "Hey, you," she says as she approaches.

"Hey yourself." I offer her the coffee. "How was your day?"

"Exhausting, but it's better now." She leans in, and I kiss her, my hand snaking around the back of her neck, holding her to me as I show her just how much I've missed her today.

"Glad to hear it."

"You seem chipper," she comments as she climbs into the driver's side, and I slip into the passenger seat.

"I've had to entertain myself by hanging out with Fearghas as he stares longingly at Eira. I'm more than chipper to be anywhere but there."

She laughs. "So it's not me but your change of scenery that has made you happy. Good to know."

"A change I wouldn't have if it weren't for you," I reply as she pulls out of the parking lot.

"Fair. I wish he'd just be honest with her. Tell her how he feels."

"Honestly? I don't know that they'll ever get there. He's afraid she'll bolt."

"Eira doesn't seem like the kind to run."

"She's been through some shit," I tell her. "A relationship is not something she's overly open to."

"That's so sad. They're both such good people."

I don't reply, though I couldn't agree more. Truthfully, I hope I'm wrong and the two of them will eventually figure out a way to find their way together, but given what I know about their situations, I won't hold my breath.

Reaching over, I thread my fingers with the free hand resting on her lap.

"What do you want to do tonight?" Rachel asks as she turns left onto the street that will take us to her apartment."

Something slams into the windshield. Glass shatters; Rachel screams, and my face impacts with something really fucking hard.

Metal groans as the car flips over and lands on its side.

Pain radiates through my body, but I manage to dematerialize onto the side of the road. Warmth trickles from my head, dripping down the side of my face as I fight to get my vision to clear.

"Rachel!" I yell. Surely she made it out of the car. My heart hammers, my head pounds.

I stumble back to the car, barely making it two feet before something hits me again. Pain blossoms in my chest, spreading through my body like wildfire. Every single inch of me is ablaze.

Every part of my body burning in a way that can only mean one thing—iron.

My vision clears as I fall to my knees. A woman stands a few yards away, her features contorted in rage as she lowers her weapon. "Didn't expect to see me again, did you?" she growls.

"What the—" I stare down at my chest, still in shock. Blood soaks the front of my shirt, the gunshot wound in my chest making it hard to draw breaths.

"Get the fuck away from him."

The dark fae turns as Rachel appears behind her. She raises her gun and fires. Rachel disappears, reappearing behind the fae. But before I can warn her, the dark fae whips out a stake and drives it into Rachel's body.

"Rachel!" I scream it, though it barely registers as more than a whisper.

She stumbles back, and the dark fae raises her gun, a sick smile on her face. "You took everything from me," she spits out. "Now, I'm going to make you watch while I take everything from you." Her gun switches targets as she swings it to me.

And fires.

Rachel rushes forward, but the bullet tears into my shoulder, and I fall backward. Rachel screams, and the woman cries out moments before a disgusting *crack* fills my ears.

Rachel comes into view above me. "Come on, Ridley, sit up."

I can't feel my legs, my arms, but I will my body to sit so I don't let her down. Tears stream down her cheeks as she tries to lift me with the iron stake in her abdomen still jutting out. "You're hurt," I choke out.

"Don't focus on me," I tell him. "We need to get you up." She places her arms underneath me and tries to lift me, but my weight is too much. "I can't dematerialize," she says, her voice panicked. "What do I do, Ridley? Tell me what to do!"

"I'll be okay," I promise her. "Because I had you." Every word sends a fresh ache through my body.

"No. You can't give up, you miserable bastard, you didn't let me, and I'm not going to let you." She closes her eyes, her arms still beneath me.

In the blink of an eye, two stunning wings spread out behind her, the deep mahogany tipped with gold the most beautiful things I've ever seen.

And then, we're flying. Wind whips over my body as she moves, and for a brief moment, I think I might just survive.

But then, the numbness overwhelms me, and my last memory is of Rachel's beautiful face bathed in the bright sunlight.

CHAPTER TWENTY

RACHEL

While my heart continues slamming against my ribs, I somehow manage to make it clear across Billings. The ground appears far too soon, though, and we slam into the gravel just outside Bronywyn's home.

"Help!" I scream as I cling to Ridley's unconscious form. Making it inside without help is not possible, especially not when I'm steadily losing blood that is trickling out around the iron stake embedded in my gut.

Removing it hadn't been an option, though, since

doing that would have led to me bleeding out a hell of a lot faster.

"Help!" I scream again, loud as I can.

A blur of movement stops in front of me, and Tarnley meets my eyes. "What happened?" He's shirtless, but he doesn't hesitate before reaching down to lift Ridley.

"We were attacked. Dark fae," I manage. My adrenaline is nothing compared to my fear, but at least we stand a chance now. If Bronywyn can get the bullets out, Tarnley can give Ridley enough blood that he will survive.

Tarnley blurs away, and I fall backward against the gravel, exhausted, bloody, and dizzy. What felt like an instant but was more than likely a few minutes later, Tarnley appears and kneels beside me.

"Ridley—"

"Bronywyn's got him now. I grabbed her before I came back out for you. You kill her?" he asks.

"Yes. Out on East Airport. You should probably send a crew out there. I totaled my car, too."

"Left quite a mess for me then, didn't you?"

I try to laugh but barely manage a sound before he's blurring us to the house, the rush like a damned roller coaster. We stop in the clinic, and he sets me down on a gurney that's already been wheeled into the room beside Ridley." Shirt open, he looks one moment away from death.

Tears blur my vision, and I force myself to look away even though it breaks my damned heart to do so.

"Bullets are out. Get him some blood." Bronywyn's tone is all business, and Tarnley leaves my side.

She hovers above me. "Any other wounds?"

"Just what happened when the car crashed," I manage through my tears.

"Okay. This is going to hurt like a son of a bitch." Her hands wrap around the iron. The gentle touch moves it enough to send a sharp pain through my abdomen.

I bite down, prepared for much, much worse.

She rips.

I scream.

"Done. Tarnley."

"On it." He appears above me and presses his wrist to my lips. Copper invades my senses, the bitter taste absorbing into my own body. Knowing I need more, I pull from his wrist, feeling my stomach rolling with the knowledge of what I'm doing.

But soon, the pain subsides, leaving me with little more than an ache.

I breathe deeply. "You okay?" Tarnley presses a cool washcloth to my forehead, and I take another breath.

"Better." I try to sit up, desperate to get a glimpse at Ridley, but Tarnley forces me back down.

"He needed substantially more," he tells me honestly. "But we've done what we can."

I nod, my throat constricting with agony as I can't

help but picture my life without the smart-ass fae I've come to be completely in love with. Truthfully, it would be no life at all.

A month ago, if someone would have told me I'd fall in love with a man I'd just met, I would have called them crazy.

But now, a life without him is far too horrific to even begin to imagine.

So, I close my eyes and pray I'll never have to experience it.

CHAPTER TWENTY-ONE

RACHEL

"Just remember to stay focused," Delaney tells her sister as she stands nervously near the door.

"Focused, got it."

"Not too late to run, you know!" Fearghas offers from outside the door.

"Will you be quiet," Eira scolds back.

"Seriously, she's already nervous enough," Magnolia, a young witch who's spent the last few months being trained in her power calls out.

Rainey glances at her appreciatively. "I'm loving the confidence, Mags."

The young witch blushes.

Rainey takes a deep breath. She's always been beautiful, though trading in her combat boots for a white silk gown certainly did her justice. Her dark hair has been pinned up on top of her head, and Delaney threaded white flowers through it. "I don't think I ever actually believed I'd be standing here," she admits. "Since you assholes kept nearly dying on me."

Delaney laughs. "Yeah, well, you're here, and you're so beautiful." She chokes up, covering her mouth with both hands.

"Easy, preggers, don't make her mascara run," Fearghas calls in.

"One more word, Fearghas," Delaney warns. "And I'll let her shoot you."

He laughs. "Don't threaten me with a good time."

Rainey turns toward me. "Well, doc?"

"You're absolutely beautiful."

She turns to Eira.

"Stunning, Rainey," she offers, looking gorgeous herself in the blood-red gown Rainey chose for her bridesmaids' dresses.

"Okay. Well." Rainey takes a deep breath and I offer her the fragrant bridal bouquet boasting roses in red and white. "I guess this is it."

I may not have known her long, but I've been

around long enough to see the hunter take out some pretty large bad guys. A modern-day superhero, she's faced down dark witches, bloodthirsty vampires, ferocious shifters, succubae, and a horde of humans with cameras pointed in her face. But not once, in all those instances, did I ever see her as panicked as she is now.

It's adorable, though I'm sure she'd shoot me for thinking so.

The door opens, and Fearghas steps through looking like an Irish *James Bond* in his tux. His eyes find Eira first, though he quickly redirects his attention to Rainey. "Astor, you are a fucking dream."

To my complete surprise, she actually blushes. Cheeks red, she shakes her head. "I swear, I don't think I've ever felt this vulnerable."

"Rainey."

She turns to her sister. "Mom and dad would be so proud."

That does it. Rainey tears up, her eyes glistening as she hugs her sister. "Thanks, Del."

After a brief moment, she straightens and carefully wipes the tears. "Well, guys, let's go get me married."

I'm up first, stepping out into the hall, holding a small bouquet of flowers. Ridley waits for me at the end of the hall, and my mouth goes dry as I drink him in. After nearly dying, I've been all but attached to him at the hip, so terrified if I let him out of my sight, he wouldn't make it back to me.

Something I know I'll have to get over, but for now, I'm simply enjoying having him in my home—and my bed.

"You are breathtaking," he says as he kisses my cheek.

"You look pretty damn good yourself."

He flashes a smile as we head to the start of our walk down the aisle. All eyes are on us as we take the careful steps toward the altar where Elijah stands, framed in a white rose archway. Bronywyn stands just behind him, ready to officiate the ceremony.

He nods kindly at me, and I return it before taking my place. Drexel and Magnolia are next, the young hunter guiding the young witch down toward me. Unsure in her heels, she trips, and he manages to keep her up on her feet. Her face turns bright red, dang near matching the dress.

As soon as she's beside me, I lean in. "I once fell flat on my face in front of the altar," I tell her. "You did good."

"Thanks, I can't believe I tripped."

"Happens to the best of us."

Eira is next, arm in arm with Tarnley as they make their way down the aisle together. The siren all but glides on heels no human should be able to wear and *not* break an ankle. Then again, she's not exactly human, is she?

Delaney and Cole come down next, Rainey's maid

of honor with her arm through that of her mates. The shifter moves slowly beside her, letting her walk—or, in this case, do the pregnant waddle—at her own pace. She looks absolutely adorable, her blood-red dress perfectly formed to her growing body.

As soon as she reaches the altar, the entire room stands on their feet. I let my gaze travel over all those in attendance, starting with the psychic detective and Rainey's partner, who is currently standing in the front row beside a massive shifter covered in tattoos. His long blonde hair is pulled back at the nape of his neck, his huge arm wrapped around the shoulders of a petite blonde to his other side.

Just behind them, Willa stands with a few shifters I don't recognize, her expression guarded. Just to her left are the only two humans in the place. Deissy leans into her fiancé, a cop at Rainey's precinct, and he presses a kiss to her temple.

Rainey steps out, and the entire room falls silent. Her arm is looped through Fearghas's as they make their way down the aisle toward Elijah, who is unable to tear his eyes from his bride. With every step she takes, her smile grows wider, and by the time she reaches him, my own cheeks hurt from the joy I'm wearing on my face.

After everything they've faced, fought for, this slice of happiness is so damned earned it makes my heart soar.

Because out of all the ugly, the blood, the fight—came this pairing and so many more.

I know it's Rainey's day, but my gaze drifts over to Ridley, who, to my surprise, is watching me.

Yes, we've seen a lot of ugly over the past few months, but there's also been love.

And isn't that exactly what we've been fighting for?

COMING SOON TO THIS WORLD...

My soul hasn't been mine for over a thousand years.

Ever since I saw her standing on that cliffside in Ireland, Eira has possessed more of me than she'll ever know. But by the time I saw her again, she'd suffered far more than anyone ever should.

She'd been broken, abused, and was unwilling to trust me no matter how many times I tried to prove my intentions.

For my kind to mate—it's rare—dangerous, which is why no one can know of my ties to the violet-eyed siren or her hold over me. My enemies would love to get their hands on the one thing that could lead to my destruction.

But when her life is threatened, I know I can't simply watch from the sidelines anymore. Not when I'm ready to rip the entire world to shreds for another moment in her presence.

. . .

COMING SOON TO THIS WORLD...

ALSO BY JESSICA WAYNE

FAE WAR CHRONICLES

EMBER IS DYING.

BUT AS SHE WILL SOON DISCOVER, SOME FATES ARE WORSE THAN DEATH.

ACCIDENTAL FAE

SIRENS BLOOD CHRONICLES

WHAT HAPPENS WHEN THE WORLD'S DEADLIEST SUPERNATURAL IS PUSHED TO HIS BREAKING POINT.

RESCUED BY THE FAE

BROKEN BY THE FAE

HEALED BY THE FAE

VAMPIRE HUNTRESS CHRONICLES

SHE'S SPENT HER ENTIRE LIFE ERADICATING THE IMMORTALS. NOW, SHE FINDS HERSELF PROTECTING ONE.

WITCH HUNTER: FREE READ

BLOOD HUNT

BLOOD CAPTIVE

BLOOD CURE

CURSE OF THE WITCH

BLOOD OF THE WITCH

Rise of the Witch

Blood Magic

Blood Bond

Blood Union

Cambrexian Realm : The Complete Series

The realm's deadliest assassin has met her match.

The Last Ward: FREE READ

Warrior Of Magick

Guardian Of Magick

Shades Of Magick

Rise of the Phoenix: The Complete Series

Ana has spent her entire life at the clutches of her enemy. Now, it's time for war.

Birth of the Phoenix

Death of the Phoenix

Vengeance of the Phoenix

Tears of the Phoenix

Rise of the Phoenix

Tethered

Sometimes, our dreams do come true. The trouble is, our nightmares can as well.

Tethered Souls

Collateral Damage

ABOUT THE AUTHOR

Photo Credit Mandi Rose Photography

USA Today bestselling author Jessica Wayne is the author of over thirty fantasy and contemporary romance novels. The latter of which she writes as J.W. Ashley. During the day, she slays laundry and dishes as a stay at home mom of three, and at night her worlds come to life on paper.

She runs on coffee and wine (as well as the occasional whiskey!) and if you ever catch her wearing matching socks, it's probably because she grabbed them in the dark.

She is a believer of dragons, unicorns, and the power of love, so each of her stories contain one of those elements (and in some cases all three).

You can usually find her in her Facebook group, Jessica's Whiskey Thieves, or keep in touch by subscribing to her newsletter.

Stay Updated:

Newsletter: https://www.jessicawayne.com/free-books-by-jessica-wayne
Website: https://www.jessicawayne.com
Readers Group: https://www.facebook.com/groups/jessicaswhiskeythieves

facebook.com/AuthorJessicaWayne
twitter.com/jessmccauthor
instagram.com/authorjessicawayne

CONTEMPORARY ROMANCE BY J.W. ASHLEY

THE CORRUPTED TRILOGY

THEY'RE BEING HUNTED AND THE ONLY WAY TO COME OUT OF IT ALIVE, IS TO PUT THEIR BADGES ASIDE.

RESCUING NORAH

SHIELDING JEMMA

TARGETING CELESTE

OLIVE YOU: *SIX BEST FRIENDS AND THEIR HUNT FOR TRUE LOVE (OR SOMETHING LIKE IT ANYWAY).*

LONG ROAD HOME: *COMING HOME WAS ALWAYS PART OF THE PLAN. HE WAS NOT.*

HOME FOR SUMMER: *HE THINKS SHE'S A SPOILED BRAT. SHE THINKS HE'S A STICK IN THE MUD. TURNS OUT, THEY'RE BOTH WRONG.*

THE LUMBERJACK EFFECT: *FACING YOUR PAST IS ALWAYS THE HARDEST PART OF MOVING FORWARD. ESPECIALLY WHEN YOU'VE KEPT A SECRET FOR FIVE YEARS.*

THE WHISKEY EFFECT: *RULE #1: NEVER GET TIED DOWN. LEO SMASHED THROUGH THAT LIKE IT WAS A PANE OF SUGAR GLASS AND HE'S AN ACTION STAR WHOSE MISSION IS TO TAKE ME DOWN...REPEATEDLY.*

Made in the USA
Columbia, SC
03 March 2022